ROBYN AND THE HOODETTES

EBONY MCKENNA

ROBYN AND THE HOODETTES

THE OUTLAW OF FOLKLORE IN A YOUNG ADULT FAIRYTALE ADVENTURE

Ebony McKenna

Printed and bound by Ingram Spark in Australia

Third Edition, 2017

ISBN 978-0-9953839-5-1

www.ebonymckenna.com

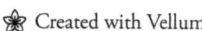 Created with Vellum

To my wonderful readers who love a rollicking adventure and a happy ever after. Huge thanks for the amazing support from the Romance Writers of Australia, and my home-grown cheer squad in the Saturday Ladies' Bridge Club; Alison, Carol, Clare, Denise, Louise, Sara and Pauline. Mega hugs to the brilliant Nicole, PhD (Awesomeness).

CHAPTER 1

NORTHERN ENGLAND, 1192 A.D.

"*R*un, girl!" Mother Eleanor said. "Run like you stole something!"

Clutching the bag of wheat in her apron, Robyn ran like a rabbit with a slathering dog on her heels. Faster, faster, her feet pounded the ground. Her chest strained. Her legs burned. Wheat seeds flew out with every thumped landing.

On she ran, away from the tax collectors who'd suddenly appeared on their outlying fields only a few minutes ago, on she ran towards the heart of her village. To the familiar buildings that would give her cover so she could hide this precious bag of grain.

Surprise shocked her into stillness. Whose carriage was that, sitting in the village green? Its panels gleamed in the autumn sunlight, its coat of arms on the door polished to a neat shine; golden stags on a sash of blue. She'd just seen that same insignia on the carriage that had pulled up next to the field they'd been ploughing and sowing. The one she'd run from. Where tax collectors were storming about demanding seventeen marks of wheat, when every villager knew they barely had ten.

And now a matching carriage sat in the middle of Loxley village, which had to mean there were more tax collectors all around her, raiding every cottage.

Not good.

Very, very, very not good.

Darting away, she raced for the safety of the barn. She slumped against the outside wall, taking huge gulps of air while trying desperately to keep quiet. Had she made too much noise?

Had anyone seen her dash to the shed? Panic swirled crazy ideas through her. She should hide inside the building. A loose section of wall was almost big enough to lift aside to crawl through. Curse her growth spurt, she'd never get in there.

It took an age for her heart to stop whacking against her ribs. With willpower and several prayers, she brought her breath half way back to normal. Throat parched, she looked ravenously towards the well for a drink. Not a chance. She'd be spotted for sure if she drew up a pail of water.

The bag of wheat was mostly safe, though. As long as nobody followed the trail of seeds to her hiding place.

Screaming and shouting filled Robyn's ears. Peering around the side of the barn, she saw armoured men helping themselves to rolls of fabric from the Miller's cottage. Men in armour? Since when did tax collectors need that level of protection?

"Oi! Put that back! You've no right!" Grannyma Miller screamed, then swatted at them with an embroidery hoop in one arm. Her wailing grandson, Tuppence, swung in her other. The hoop broke into splinters on the tax collector's helmets, but to Robyn's relief, Grannyma did not hit them with Tuppence. With another yell of defiance, Grannyma ripped the fully-loaded swaddling off the babby and flung it at them. The stinky bomb missed its target and splattered on the ground. The smell carried all the way to the barn where Robyn had to breathe through her already desiccated mouth so she didn't retch.

Fearing nobody, the men turned their backs on Grannyma and her screaming babby, then sauntered into the blacksmith's hut like they owned it. Most likely to help themselves to whatever was in there.

An ache Robyn couldn't name welled in her chest. If only her father were here, he'd know what to do. How to handle this. But her father wasn't here to protect Loxley. Neither were the rest of the men in the village. Not since they'd marched off under the king's banner of three golden lions on a red field, to join something called a crusade.

Leaving Loxley defenceless.

Anger overrode Robyn's instinct to hide, as she watched these men take whatever they wanted. The dirty, filthy thieves! How dare they! Red mist clouded her vision. They were acting like thieves, not taxmen. Maybe they'd stolen those shiny carriages and were only pretending to be tax collectors? She had to do something. Anything. To save her village.

Making sure the strangers were well inside the smithy, Robyn crept in the other direction towards the carriage and made friends with the two horses attached to it.

"Easy there. Easy."

Such fine horseflesh, their coats fair gleamed. They were shod and everything. These horses were used to taking the high road, not the low dales. A plan formed in Robyn's mind, but it meant parting with some of the precious grain. If she had time to think of anything else, she would, but time was in desperately short supply. She plunged her hand into the bag of grain in her apron and offered half a palm full to one horse, then the other. They'd need a quick burst of energy in a moment.

Sneaking between the beasts, Robyn found the belts connecting the harness to the carriage and wiggled them free. Now the tax collectors could load as much as they wanted, but the carriage would go nowhere.

Somebody had left a hooded travelling cloak on the driver's seat. Robyn slipped it over her shoulders and tied the fastener. Now the men wouldn't see her face if they spotted her.

With a quick shake of her hands to steady the nerves, Robyn set to untying the rest of the harness buckles and belts, setting the horses free.

"Now scram!" she said.

They didn't budge.

Any other horse or cow-even pig-would have leapt at the chance of freedom. These animals were so placid, so tame . . . so stupid, they went on munching and standing so stupidly still. Panic made Robyn desperate. These horses had to move, and quickly.

Maybe a shove from behind would help? She climbed onto the front of the carriage, to the driver's seat.

"You there!" One of the men said.

Uh-oh, they were out of the smithy, ready to load up their stolen stuff. Terrified, Robyn put the bag of wheat safely on the driver's seat for now, then threw herself onto the back of one horse, her long dark hair flinging over her eyes, making it hard to see. She grabbed onto the mane and clamped her knees in tightly.

"Yar!"

Nothing. Not even a wobble from the animal below her. An animal that smelled of soap and little work. Not like the cows in the field that filled the air with dung, sweat and dust.

"Get down lad!" The man dropped his bounty and charged for Robyn.

Running hot and cold from worry and excitement, Robyn yelled, "Giddyup!"

Still nothing!

A man's hard hand grabbed her by the boot. She kicked out in defence; her boot flew off but so did his hand. Her foot sprang back onto the horse's flank. Startled, the beast shot off like an loosed arrow and charged. The other horse made a whinny and cantered after them. Robyn kept her body low, fists clenched in the mane, knees pressed in hard to keep balance. Only now did she remember she had absolutely no idea how to control a horse.

Left a bit.

Right a bit.

Bad wobble. Hang on!

Don't fall off! Quick correction.

Onwards the horse galloped, Robyn twisted her grip into its mane. Thump thump, tha-thump, thump. The hooves hitting the ground matched Robyn's pulse. On the animal raced, up into the wooded hills and further into the Shire Wood.

After her initial panic wore off, and she'd not fallen off, Robyn began to notice something of a pattern in the horse's gait and she could anticipate the rhythm of bumps and thumps. Growing more confident as they reached the crest of a hill, she shifted her weight to look back. The hood of her cloak flipped onto her head, blocking the edges of her vision, but she saw enough of Loxley down below.

Free from its harness, the other horse had bolted away, towards the village wheat field. Relief sagged her body. Maybe the men would catch the other stray horse before they came after her? At least she had a great head start on them.

They did have the bag of grain though; the bag Robyn had left behind in her panic. She could have smacked herself. She had one job, to protect that bag, and she'd failed. Now, through the gap in the trees, she saw what her actions cost. Curse it! A man upended the bag and tipped the seeds all over the ground.

Of all the disrespectful, wasteful things to do! Robyn gritted her teeth in anger and failure. She was in charge of protecting that grain, it might have been all the winter wheat the village had left to plant. She should have hidden it in the shed, but no, she'd left it out in the open.

"You are such an idiot!" she said through gritted teeth.

The horse made a weird sound.

"Not you, horse. Me. I'm the idiot."

She couldn't look at the village any more, didn't want to see the wanton destruction. Also, her foot was cold from losing her boot, but that was the least of her issues right now.

Robyn urged the horse into the wood. As the animal slowed to a trot, then walked at an even pace, Robyn's blank, adrenalin-filled head let some proper thoughts through. Useful thoughts. Constructive, practical thoughts.

There was no way those men in the village were real tax collectors. Not with the way they were being so wasteful. After all, would tax collectors demand seventeen marks of wheat, then tip half a mark into the ground? Not likely. Maybe they'd stolen the carriages, then gone on a raiding spree? They were only pretending to represent the Sheriff, so they could take advantage of unprotected villages like hers.

For a moment, smug satisfaction filled Robyn with righteous indignation. Then a new thought crashed hard on the previous one. What if they really had been tax collectors after all? Just a little brutal and stupid about it?

That would mean Robyn had stolen a crown horse.

She'd hang for theft if they caught her.

OK, she had to make sure she wasn't caught. Which meant getting off the horse right now. After all, it would be pretty hard to claim you weren't a horse thief if you were caught riding it at the time.

Any stranger would know by her roughly woven clothes and boots–OK, one boot now–that she was a peasant; the magnificent animal she rode could not possibly belong to her.

Therefore, if she and the horse parted ways, she could wait it out amongst the birch trees and fallen leaves of the Shire Wood, then sneak back to Loxley under cover of darkness. Nobody would be any the wiser.

Unless the thieving men . . . who might very well be legitimate tax collectors . . . had seen her face and recognized her?

Wait! Hadn't they called her "lad" at some point?

Maybe they'd be looking for a boy, not a girl?

That could work!

Robyn took her chance and slid off. She landed hard on her bottom and winced with pain. The horse stopped and turned its head, its nostrils flaring as it sniffed the air.

"You're free now, off you trot."

The horse lifted its top lip and kept sniffing. Then she pushed her lips onto Robyn's head and nibbled at her hair. From her position sitting on the ground, Robyn could clearly see the horse was lacking the necessary equine equipment to be called a boy.

"Get off!" Robyn said, pulling away and smoothing her hair down. Ewwww, horse spit! Her hair clumped into dark ribbons as she tried to clean it. Meanwhile, the beast took a step sideways, but didn't walk off.

"Fine then, I'll go." Robyn rose and had a good look around. In the distance, she heard the splash of a stream over rocks. Water! She was gasping for a drink. The river would be at the bottom of the hill. Walking hurt her one-unshod-foot as mud and sticks jabbed at her sole, but she had tough skin and she could wash her foot in the stream.

Memories of rabbit hunting with her father assailed her. They'd drank where the rabbits drank, knowing the water would be fresh and life-giving. As she neared the river, Robyn's ears pricked up. Hers were not the only footsteps in the woods.

"No way!" she looked back to see the horse following her, like a shadow. "Shoo, shoo!" She waved her arms.

The horse whickered and lifted her head, but didn't go.

"This day gets worse!" Robyn turned her back on the animal and made for the stream. All the exertion had made her thirsty. Maybe the horse was thirsty too? Of course! That must be why it was following her. It had been pulling a carriage all day and had just carried her off into the thickets at a fast clip.

The stream flowed slowly when they reached the banks. It trickled over rocks but otherwise looked brown and oozy, not at all refreshing. Robyn (with the horse-shadow behind her) kept walking until the water flowed swiftly over rocks. Two startled rabbits darted off. Here the stream looked clear and bright. Refreshing.

Robyn crouched at the bank and began scooping the water into her mouth with her palms, as her father had taught her. It soothed her throat and filled her belly. The horse waded into the water and slurped with contentment. Taking a moment, she sat on the banks of the river in a pile of dried fallen leaves. Checking her foot, it was dirty but the sticks and stones of the Shire Wood hadn't broken the skin. The horse would find its way home. Didn't they always? Or was that merely one of Grannyma Miller's old sayings? In any case, Robyn had to keep moving. It was too dangerous to risk being found with the animal.

"Thank you for the ride, Horse, but I have to be going. Alone." She followed the riverbank downstream, biding her time until dusk.

Splash, splash, splash-splash.

There were hooves in the water, following her.

"Take a hint, Horse." Robyn waved her arms in the air, trying to shoo her away again.

The horse only stepped closer, nodded her head and then rubbed her cheek against Robyn's arm.

7

So friendly. Robyn rubbed the horse's nose with affection. "You are a sweet thing, but you're going to land me into trouble."

"I'll say." A big hand landed hard on her shoulder, anchoring her to the ground.

With a gulp, Robyn turned to face her captor.

CHAPTER 2

*R*obyn looked up into the face of a giant. Her knees buckled, not with fear but relief.

"Oh, it's you! I thought it was the Sheriff's man!" she said, looking into the smiling eyes of her friend, Joan.

Joan stood higher up the bank than Robyn, but even if they'd been on level ground the young woman would have towered over her. Joan lived in Littleton, the next village downstream from Loxley. It was a tiny dot of a place, hence the name.

"I like your new horse," Joan said in her booming voice.

"Not so loud! I don't want to be found!"

"Sorry!" Joan said in a whisper that frightened squirrels.

Joan was a foundling, which was obvious to everyone who met her parents. Joan's hair had the colour of freshly baled hay, while her parents' heads were as orange as fire. Coupled with her parents' short stature, they'd never been able to pass off the statuesque Joan as their own. Secretly Robyn wondered if Joan's first parents might be giants.

Despite Joan's scary size, the horse gave a snort of approval and snuggled in for a pat on the nose.

"She's not mine." Robyn said. "I can't be seen with her. We can't be seen with her."

"She sure acts like she's yours."

9

Robyn sighed. "I stole her."

Joan raised her brows.

"But I didn't mean to! We were out in the field doing all the jobs the men usually do, but they're not back yet, obviously, and then a carriage turned up and all these men got out and said we had to pay seventeen marks of wheat in taxes and–"

"Slow down." Joan held her spade-like palms up. "The men in the carriage. Did it have a coat of arms with a blue sash?"

"And three golden stags on it." Robyn had taken an interest in heraldry, ever since her father had marched off under the King's red banner with its golden lions. She'd been keeping an eye out for its return ever since.

"Sounds like the same men who raided Littleton this morning. Took all the chickens they could carry. Left us with the old boilers. The place is so covered in feathers you'd think the sky was falling. Sounds like they hit us up and then moved on to you."

"They said they were acting on behalf of the Sheriff of Nottingham. We've had tax collectors before, but they were never that brutal." Robyn said.

"Maybe the crusade's going badly," Joan said. "Speaking of, any word from your Dad?"

"Not yet." Nostalgia pierced Robyn as she remembered the fun she and her father used to have. Her memories glossed over all the times they'd argued or she'd been in trouble. "Not even a carrier pigeon in six months. What about your cousin?"

At least Joan still had both her parents, elderly as they might be.

"Nothing from him either," Joan said as she moved in to give the horse a good pat on the neck. Robyn and Joan both shut up about the people they missed the most. They had a way of almost talking about the things and people they cared for, before they found a way to change the subject.

Joan looked longingly at the horse. "She sure is a beautiful thing."

"I told her to shoo, but she's harder to lose than a shadow."

"Hello Shadow, I'm Joan, lovely to meet you."

"Don't give her a name!" Robyn threw her hands up in desperation. "I'm trying to get rid of her! Oh come on, stop with the cuddles!"

"But she's beautiful. And she smells so nice."

"I know!" Robyn moved in for a smooch, inhaling the horse's scent. "But honestly, she's far too pretty. If anyone saw us, they'd know we'd stolen her."

"Then we have to make her look like she does belong," Joan said with a gleam in her eye. "Come on, let's give her an un-bath."

With a giggle of conspiracy, they lead Shadow into the stream and proceeded to splash water on her, then they mussed up her gleaming coat and mane by brushing her the wrong way. It had to be done. No peasant could possibly possess such a fine horse.

"Nagging her up. What a shame. Feels worse than when I spilt mead all over mother's tapestry," Joan said.

"What about the shoes?" Robyn asked as she smeared mud on Shadow's fetlock.

Joan winked. "We'll take her to your handsome blacksmith later, get them taken off. By the way, did you lose a boot or find one?"

"It . . . fell off," Robyn said, her brain catching on Joan's description of her *handsome* smith. "I hope those ratbags have left something for Marion to work with."

"He's a clever man, that one," Joan said. "He'll work something out."

"Do you fancy him or something?" Robyn said with a grin. "You do, don't you? You really fancy him!"

"Not half as much as you do!" Joan shot back.

"I do not!"

"Liar!"

They threw water and mud at each other. A fair amount landed on the horse, which helped make the three of them look miserably poor and dirty. Both Robyn's feet were soaked numb from the cold water.

All of which distracted Robyn from thinking too much about Marion. He'd always been a kid in Robyn's eyes, although he was barely a season younger than her. On the other hand, he was probably the oldest lad left in the village.

Did that automatically make him a man as Joan had called him?

Robyn and Joan stood back to admire their mudwork. Shadow looked like she'd been ridden hard and put away wet. But there was no disguising the fact she was a superior horse with regal standing, not some village nag.

"We could always say we found her, that we're trying to find her owners," Joan said.

Robyn nodded.

"D'you think the tax collectors are gone yet?" Joan asked.

"One way to find out," Robyn said. "Come on Shadow."

The horse and the two girls made their way towards Loxley. Darkness crept into the sky, so they keep close to the King's Road to avoid getting lost.

"What's that?" Joan said, grabbing Robyn's arm.

She heard it too, noises made by hooves and people. Possibly a carriage or two judging from the creaky-wheely sounds. Heading straight for them.

"Hide!" Robyn said.

They made a dash for the shrubs growing beside the road. They must have been young holly bushes, for they still had green leaves but they were spiky and bit into her bare foot.

The Sheriff's horses, pulling two carriages behind them like a double trailer, came into view.

That's when Robyn cursed the horse afresh. The dense beast stood on the road, in full view. Whisper-shouting, Robyn called out, "Get down here!"

Oh that horse, she's going to be the death of me.

Hiding in the shrubbery, Joan whispered "Stay here", then she grabbed a tree branch, pulled her hood over her head and hobbled out to the road pretending to be years older.

"There ye are ye great nag." She did something to her voice to sound like an oldie as well.

"Ho there!" A man's voice said.

"Ho-ho to you," Joan answered, sounding confident and jolly.

Knees folded awkwardly under her chin, Robyn heard a series of creaks from the timber as several men climbed down from the carriages to get a better look at Joan. Any second now they would take back their horse. Oh no! What if they accused Joan of stealing Shadow? She had to do something to help her friend.

"Get your stinking nag off the King's Road!" A man ordered.

Wait, what? Could these men not tell a prime horse from a hack?

"Go on, off with you!" Another voice said, cracking in the middle. It sounded like a really young lad who was trying to sound older, as if willing his voice to break.

Through the shrubbery, Robyn saw the shapes of five . . . no, seven men . . . walking towards Joan to get her and the animal out of their way.

"She's only got one other speed, and it's slower," Joan said, adding that wheeze old people made so well.

The way Joan acted, maybe her first parents hadn't been giants after all, but travelling minstrels. Seeing how distracted the men were, Robyn grew emboldened. As silently as possible, she crept towards the second carriage. Someone had roughly attached it to the first carriage so they could haul it with them. Would they tow it all the way to Nottingham? According to the map her father had once scratched out on her cottage floor –"Not to scale, you under-stand," he'd said–Nottingham was a whole day's ride away. Sheffield was closer, although Robyn had never been there either.

Joan was still talking on the road up ahead, but it wouldn't be long before the men returned to the carriages. Sneaking a peek inside, Robyn saw the sacks of wheat they'd taken from her village. Sacks of milled flour were in here too, along with a roll of fabric from the Miller cottage, and Marion's tools. Things that rightly belonged to Loxley.

Whoever had attached the second carriage hadn't done a very good job. With a few quiet tugs and twists, she untied the connecting rope. Heaving all her weight against it, she managed to push the fully laden carriage five steps before something snapped with a horrendous crack.

"What the devil?" One of the men shouted.

Robyn grabbed the first thing she could reach and swung it around hard. It connected with a man's stomach; he fell to the ground with a grunt. Whoa, that was easy! Then Robin noticed she'd whacked him with Marion's blacksmith hammer. No wonder he'd gone down with the first swing.

More thwacks and whacks filled the air.

"Joan!" Robyn raced towards the sound of snapping wood and shouting people. Poor Joan, it would be six against one. The poor girl didn't stand a–

"Who hoo!" Joan swung her branch like a long staff, whacking the men into each other. They staggered backwards, regained their footing, then bolted for the safety of the front carriage, locking themselves in.

"Come back and fight me!" Joan said as she bashed her stick against the door.

Looking around, Robyn saw four men sprawled on the road, each of them groaning or holding their palms up in surrender.

"Get on your wagon," Joan roared at them, "Or you'll feel the force of my weapon on your softest parts."

Wounded and miserable, the men rose on unsteady feet and climbed aboard the front of the carriage.

"Did I get them all?" Joan asked. Her face split with a grin that shone in the dim light.

"There's one more up the back, I got him with this." Robyn held Marion's hammer. A hammer that felt so much heavier now that the excitement had worn off. "He doesn't look too steady. We might need to load him in."

They walked to the wounded man and rolled him over. He refunded his stomach, blerking diced parsnips onto the road. Robyn pulled his boots off to take for herself. They were far too big for her feet, but she could cram some wool into the toes when she reached home.

Together she and Joan carried the messy man to the front carriage and made the rest of the crew haul him aboard. He regurgitated again, filling the air with acrid smells.

"He's your problem now," Joan said.

Shadow finally moved off the road and nibbled at a clump of grass. As if she knew her work was done. Robyn and Joan walked to the horses at the front of the carriage and checked their harnesses were tied. All good, according to Joan, who then gave the closest one a good slap on the rump.

"Giddyup!" Unlike Shadow, these horses knew when it was time to push off. Soon the horses, the defeated men and their carriage trundled off down the King's Road and into the night.

Leaving Joan, Robyn and Shadow with a carriage to haul back to the village.

"We did it!" Joan held her hand aloft for a high five. Robyn had to jump to reach it.

"We got our answer," Robyn said as they strolled towards the horseless wagon. When the fight was on, there had been no time for the luxury of reflection. Now there was far too much time for guilt to settle in.

Joan stalled. "What was the question?"

Regret twisted Robyn's stomach. "They're definitely the Sheriff's men. Proper thieves would have fought harder."

"Thanks a lot!"

"You know what I mean," Robyn said as she encouraged Shadow towards the carriage so they could strap her in for their return trip. "They were good and proper tax collectors, and now we're in a whole world of trouble."

CHAPTER 3

*T*he darkness made it difficult to see anything other than vague shapes. If not for Shadow guiding them along, Robyn would have stumbled off into the shrubbery. When they made it back to Loxley, they found a bonfire burning in the middle of the green and just about everyone from the village standing around it.

"Robyn?" Mother Eleanor stood up and peered towards them. "Robyn!" Her mother charged towards her, crying out, "You're here, you're safe!" Eleanor smothered Robyn in a fierce hug and didn't let go.

"What's going on?" Robyn managed to squeeze out.

"You're alive! I thought they'd taken you!" Eleanor splattered Robyn's face with wet kisses.

"I'm fine, Mother, relax. I owe it all to Shadow here."

Eleanor took a step back and noticed the horse. Uh-oh. Time for some sweet talk. "She followed me home. Can I keep her?"

"Oh, Robyn . . . I don't know. We can't bring a horse into the cottage. For starters, where would we put the cow?"

The animals, including a cow, three goats and an ever-changing number of chickens, lived on the lower level. Robyn and her mother had their straw bed in the alcove above.

"She saved me. Twice. Once in the village when we escaped and the second time on the King's Road."

"But Robyn dear, she must be a noble horse–" Eleanor suddenly noticed Joan. "Oh my!"

Joan stepped forward and pulled her hood back to reveal her smiling face.

"It's you, Joan." Eleanor patted her palm to her chest. "I didn't recognize you with that hood on. Come here then and give me a hug."

While Eleanor and Joan embraced, the rest of the villagers crowded around them, admiring the fine horse and the incredible carriage.

Little Madge the Miller's daughter wandered up. She was only a season younger than Robyn, but her slight frame made the age gap look like years.

"We'll have to get rid of these," Madge said, looking at the distinctive coat of arms on the side panels. "My Grannyma says they belong to the Earl of Derby."

They'd stolen from an Earl?

Clods of earth filled Robyn's belly. The entire village would hang at this rate. "Get Marion and see if he can melt it down into something."

"I would if I had the tools."

Robyn spun around to see Marion, smiling at her. He looked . . . different in the evening light. The glow of the bonfire cast light over his cheeks and neck, emphasizing the planes and shadows. He'd cut his dusty brown hair short again, probably done it himself judging from the uneven chops and curls.

"I like your hair like that," Joan said, giving him an appreciative nod.

"Kind of had to," Marion rubbed the ground with his toe and then looked back to the smithy hut.

"You didn't burn yourself?" Joan asked.

Marion ran his hand through his hair and said, "Not much."

Robyn mentally kicked herself for staring at him.

Clearing his throat, Marion said, "Good thing you got home when you did, Robby, we were about to send out a search party."

The use of his pet name for her made Robyn smile. "I've got a surprise for you." She opened the carriage door and Marion's stolen tools fell to the ground with clangs and clunks.

"Nice one!" he lunged at them, grateful to have them back.

"But wait, there's more!" Robyn had never felt so blessed and prideful as she pulled out sack after sack of wheat and milled flour. Supplies they needed to survive the oncoming winter. She handed the bags to the rightful owners who giggled and cried out with glee.

It felt pretty darn wonderful to be bringing their food, tools and fabric back where they belonged. "Three cheers for Joan, she did the heavy lifting!" Robyn said. "She took on five men with only a stick in her hand!"

The villagers cheered for Joan and Robyn. No need to tell them the men were working for the Sheriff of Nottingham. That would only complicate things and cause undue worry. Wouldn't it?

Marion returned for the rest of his tools. "I'm firing up the forge, we'd better get the livery off tonight, just in case anyone comes by in the morning."

"Good idea!" Robyn said, then turned to the crowd. "Everyone?"

Nobody paid her any attention. They were all too excited.

"Everyone!" She shouted this time. They stopped and looked up to her. Yikes, her throat turned dry so she swallowed. "We can't celebrate yet. We need to get the fire burning hot in the forge and melt down everything that could belong to the Earl of Derby. I thought the tax men who came here were thieves, that they'd stolen the Earl's carriages. We've had plenty of tax collectors in the past, but they've never behaved like those men did."

Lots of nods.

"But in truth," which Robyn now had to explain, past the clump in her throat, "The reason they're using the Earl's carriage is because they really were tax collectors and they had the Earl of Derby's blessing."

Gasps spread through the crowd.

"We're going to be all right." Robyn splayed her palms out to keep everyone calm. "We just need to be quick and work together and we'll all be fine. We need to remove the Earl's colours, and get the iron shoes off the horse. Her name's Shadow, and she kept me safe all this time."

The village became a blur of activity. Through all the cheering and excitement, Shadow didn't seem the slightest bit fussed. But when Marion came to lead her towards the smithy, Shadow wasn't having any of it.

Robyn climbed down from the carriage and made her way to the horse. "Easy girl. It's for your own good."

The soothing tones didn't calm Shadow. The horse would not take one step towards Marion's workshop and its forge, glowing bright in the dark night.

Shadow stepped backwards, snorting contempt.

"Fine then, we'll deal with the carriage first," Marion said, taking a chisel out of his leather apron and wedging it behind the coat of arms.

"All right Shadow, you win this round," Robyn said, leading the horse towards the cottage she shared with her mother and animals. "Now, in you get, and don't upset Bella. She's a temperamental one, that cow, and if she gets in one her moods we won't get any milk."

All of which Robyn expected Shadow to understand not a jot, but she said it anyway because when Shadow later upset Bella, she could say "I told you so" to the horse. Just as her mother often said to her.

With Shadow tucked away behind the half-high door, Robyn turned back to the village to see the glow of the smithy and sparks flying out of the chimney.

The children were having fun vandalizing the carriage. Hopefully it would still work as a carriage when they were through with it.

Above them, the stars twinkled through gaps in the cloud. The cool wind kissed Robyn's cheeks, reminding her of the cold season to come.

If she hadn't done what she'd done, her village would have faced starvation. But now that she'd done what she had–with Joan's help– would they be bringing the Sheriff of Nottingham's wrath upon them?

The clang and thunk of heavy tools drew Robyn towards the forge, where Marion worked the metal like a master craftsman. He'd put on thick leather sleeves over his arms to protect them from sparks.

"So they weren't a band of outlaws after all," Marion said as he clanged and banged away.

Robyn grew defensive. "But they sure acted like it."

"They're bound to come back," he said, not helping her guilty conscience one bit.

Robyn shrugged, trying to brave away her misery.

"Word will get to the Sheriff soon enough, so we'd better be ready," Marion said. A stray spark flew onto his head and he swatted it down. The smell of singed hair mixed with hot iron filled the air.

Smithing used to be something Marion's grandfather and father had done, but they were off at the war, too, just like Robyn's father. Marion's two older brothers had gone as well. Robyn wondered if she'd had brothers, whether they would have gone too.

Hanging from hooks all the way across the ceiling were the myriad tools that clanged and chimed when the wind roared through. Tongs, hammers, more tongs but smaller than the other ones, things that looked like hammers but must have been something else. Gaps where more tools should have been but weren't yet put away.

"Hey Robyn, look what I made the other day," Marion said. He took something down from the shelf behind him. "What do you think?"

"It's beautiful." Turning it over she saw something stamped into the base.

"That's my new hallmark, two letter Ms, it stands for "Marion Made",' he said with a satisfied grin as he took one of his sleeves off. To reveal his toned arm beneath.

Robyn felt heat spread over her face. It had to be from the forge. Who knew he was developing so . . . interestingly.

"I know what letters they are," she said, sounding far too defensive. Because she had to say something to cover for the fact she'd been staring at him. Time to change the topic. "The base is round, how can the bowl rest on the table?"

"It's not a bowl, you trout, it's a helmet. I haven't put the ear protectors on yet. Here." He took the helmet back and placed it on his head. "See? Perfect for when I go to the crusades."

Robyn's voice rose an octave. "You're not joining the war!" Why did the thought of him leaving upset her so? Was it because she too wanted an adventure and didn't want to be left behind? That must be it.

"Hush up!" Marion hissed as he wiped the perspiration off his arm and put the sleeve back in place.

Darn. She'd been enjoying the view.

Then he got back to the forge, pumping the bellows to bring the heat up, creating extra noise to drown them out. Robyn stepped in closer. The heat of the forge roasted the side of her body. "You are not going on the crusades. If you got hurt, Mother Mary would kill you."

"Which is why you're not going to tell her," Marion shot back.

Worries lurched in her belly. "But you can't! You're the only one who knows how to use–" Robyn cast her hands out "–all this!"

He pumped the bellows, "So it's not that you'd miss me or anything?"

"What?"

Marion charged the bellows again. "See if the children are finished ripping off the carriage."

Feelings in a muddle, Robyn ventured away from Marion.

Outside by the carriage, the children were having too much fun.

"They're so pretty, can we keep them?" Madge showed Robyn the decorative badges they'd chiselled off the carriage doors. The insides were looking bare as well, as the children stripped away curtains and cushions.

"No, we can't keep any of it. Take every last scrap of metal to Marion so he can melt it down. I'm sure he'll make you new toys if you ask nicely." Actually, Robyn wasn't sure at all, but she had to say something encouraging to the children for their quick work. "No Issie, don't take the wheels off, we don't have enough blocks to chock underneath it." A wheel-less carriage on blocks in the middle of the village green? Not the kind of ornament the village's stern Grannymas would appreciate.

A familiar snuffling noise sounded behind her. Turning, Robyn saw Shadow standing there. For a horse, she looked pretty sheepish.

"You're not supposed to be here," Robyn said. "How did you get out anyway?" Through the flickering firelight, she saw the half-door to her cottage wide open and a bewildered-looking Bella the cow wondering if it were morning yet.

"Come on Shadow, back to bed."

Shadow nuzzled her arm.

The days' events were catching up with Robyn. Tiredness made the decision for her. "It's time for sleep, come on."

The horse had the good sense to follow her home and Robyn checked the latch was attached to the door. Still there, so it wasn't broken. Had she not clicked it shut properly last time, or had the horse worked out how to open it?

The cow began lowing. "No Bella, back to sleep for you as well."

"The village is so proud of you, sweetheart," Eleanor said, jogging up with Joan by her side. In the darkness, Joan looked so tall, she could have been the parent and Eleanor the child. Her mother added, "Joan's bunking in with us tonight."

"Sure," Robyn said as weariness made her yawn.

"I was so worried. What happened to you out there?" Eleanor asked as the three of them made their way into the cottage and climbed the ladder into the shared straw bed.

"It's all a blur," Robyn said as she relayed the story to her mother. She got some events in the wrong order so Joan took over narration duties.

"What an adventure," Eleanor said when they'd finished.

Really? In the heat of the moment, Robyn hadn't noticed. But now that someone else had said it, she felt a thrill move through her.

Adventure.

Kind of nice to think she'd had one. But all the same, it wasn't anything compared the kind of adventures her father would be having.

"Mother, is the Earl of Derby working for the Sheriff of Nottingham?"

"No dear, the Earl of Derby is the Sheriff of Nottingham."

Robyn's stomach curdled like milk left in the sun. Once the Earl-Sheriff found out what she'd done, he'd send his anger down on their village like a swarm of bees.

"Get to sleep dear," Eleanor said.

Robyn sighed. "I'm trying. But mother, what's going to happen next?"

"I don't know." Now it was her mother's turn to sigh. "But I do know that not getting any sleep won't make things any better."

Her mother's advice made perfect sense, but it still didn't help. Today she'd made a powerful enemy. Would the Sheriff-Earl send his men to punish Robyn, or the whole village?

To ENSURE the bags of grain couldn't be taken from them again, the villagers took to the fields the next morning and got busy planting. If the Sheriff's men wanted the wheat back, they'd have to sift the soil to get it. Joan was a marvel with the plough, being strong enough to steer the device in a straight line. The grannymas were also out, raking the soil to a fine tilth and covering the seeds. They'd brought all the babbies with them and had sat them under a tree, where they rolled about and played in the crunchy fallen leaves.

Marion and Madge did something pretty clever. They had several light planks of wood, which they attached together with straps of leather to form a pen to keep the babbies in.

"They look like piglets," Joan said as she completed another long, straight, plough line.

"They look like they're having fun," Robyn said, at which point, Madge's little brother Tuppence toppled backwards into a pile of leaves.

Everyone was so busy laughing at the delightful babbies' antics, they didn't realize how much work they were getting done. By mid-afternoon they were finished and the villagers offered Joan and Robyn more food than they could possibly get through in a week of dinners.

"Come on you," Mother Eleanor said as the afternoon wore on. "We should get Joan back to Littleton before her parents worry where she's got to. A good walk will do you good."

Joan managed a groaning few steps before she had to rest against the side of the village well.

Eleanor gasped, "Don't lean too hard, Joan, that well's not–"

"Whoa!" The top stones came loose and Joan reeled backwards.

"–sturdy." Eleanor made a pantomime sigh.

"Take this with you." Grannyma Miller shoved a sack of flour into Robyn's arms.

Umpfh. Heavy stuff. Did she have to carry it the whole way? Her arms would drop off at this rate.

With the villagers' farewells carrying on the breeze, Robyn, Joan and Eleanor turned their backs on Loxley and headed towards Littleton. Shadow made a bee-line for Robyn and walked beside her. A moment later, Robyn and Joan realized it was silly to toil with the bags when they had horse right there, so they slung their load on to Shadow's back.

Only a short walk–an hour, tops–the cottages on the outskirts of Littleton came into view.

"Lord above," Eleanor said. "I remember when all this was fields."

The bend in the road opened to reveal the main buildings in the village. Feathers galore were blown like autumn leaves into drifts. The Sheriff's men sure had made a mess of things.

Hardly big enough to be a village, Littleton boasted a few small cottages with kitchen gardens at the front and fields behind. But Littleton had something Loxley did not: A stone tower keep, taller than the mighty oaks that reached bare arms towards the top of it. It was completely out of place amongst all the thatched-roof cottages. A single, square building with arched doorways below and sawtooth battlements along the top of each wall. Too small for a church (although the entire village could fit inside it), it looked like somebody had started building a castle years ago, but their ambitions had surpassed their abilities.

"Come on, let's put this away," Joan said, taking the bags of flour towards the tower.

Inside the stone walls they found a ladder leading upwards to a trapdoor. The ladder creaked and groaned as Joan climbed up with the sack over her shoulder. Robyn thought it best to wait until Joan was all the way up on the next floor before climbing herself. Who knew if the timber would hold both their weight?

The acrid stench of chicken poo and stale air assaulted her as she stepped through. Time to breathe through the mouth.

"If you don't mind, I'll stay down here with Shadow," Mother said.

Smart woman.

Joan climbed up yet another ladder, heading towards a trap door in the opposite corner.

"Can't we leave the bags here?" Robyn asked.

"This is where we put the chickens every night, so the foxes can't get them. If you put the food in here, the chickens will eat it all."

True. But the chickens would get fat and delicious, Robyn thought. "Where are the chickens, by the way?"

"Dunno. Probably scratching for worms down by the river."

Taking the next ladder up, balancing her own bag of flour, Robyn came through to the third floor. No sun came in here at all. The arched windows on each of the four walls had all been boarded up to keep out the rain and the wind.

"Over here," Joan said, laying down her load.

Robyn did the same. "I can never get over how quiet it is here."

"Yeah . . ." Joan said, then a strange look came over her face–it was hard to tell in the darkness. "It is quiet, isn't it?"

Too quiet. Joan climbed the last ladder and opened the final trapdoor to the sky above. Light and fresh air streamed through. Blinking, Robyn hauled herself up to the top deck, where she found herself eye-level with the skeleton branches of the tree tops.

"Where is everyone?" Joan said, looking out across all four corners of the tower.

Fear sliced into Robyn as she too gazed over the empty fields, shading her eyes from the late autumn sun. The villagers of Littleton should be sowing their winter wheat as well. Or at the very least, someone should be watching the chickens.

Even the chickens were quiet. No, they hadn't gone quiet, they'd simply gone. Along with everyone else in the village.

"Something's happened," Joan said, making for the trap door to climb down again.

Robyn gulped. Her gaze took another lap of the battlements, searching for signs of people. Looking back towards Loxley, she saw movement on the mud road. Someone was running towards the town. A male, with even strides, pumping arms and a chest broader than she remembered. It looked like Marion. With parchment in his hand as he ran towards them.

Robyn scuttled to the bottom of the tower just as Marion reached them.

"The Sheriff's men are back," he said, between huffs and puffs as he tried to collect his breath. "They're making us evacuate." Huff, puff, pant, wheeze. "They made up some story about the Shire Wood being full of thieves so they're moving us on to Sheffield for our own protection."

Panic flinched her muscles. They thought the woods were full of thieves? But the thieves were only Robyn and Joan. And anyway, they weren't thieves; they were merely taking back what was theirs in the first place.

"Look," Marion unrolled the parchment. It had tears in the corners where he'd ripped it off the barn wall they'd nailed it to. "See what it says?"

"I can read!" Robyn ground out. "They've just written it in a weird way, that's all."

Robyn sort of recognized the angry slash of the letters written along the top of the paper, but the rest of the words swam about on the page. If she concentrated, really concentrated . . . she still couldn't read it.

Joan asked, "What's this about 'hoded men'?"

"Hooded," Marion corrected. "They're saying the woods are full of hooded men."

"Where?" Joan asked.

"I think they mean us," Robyn said, pressing her lips together in thought. "They mustn't have got a good look at our faces."

Joan looked offended. "They thought I was a man? Honestly, I did a fine job of sorting them out and they're not even giving me the credit for it!"

"Hang on a minute. This could work in our favour." Robyn said.

"You're thinking what I'm thinking then," Marion said.

Robyn nodded. "They're looking for a band of men, not a couple of girls."

"Young ladies, please." Joan looked thoroughly annoyed at this development.

"A couple of very strong ladies that handed them their backsides," Marion added for good measure.

Nice save, Robyn thought.

Eleanor butted in. "And they've moved everyone out?"

"To Sheffield. They're saying it's for our own good, but it's bull–"

"–Marion!" Eleanor said, sounding like everyone's mother.

"Sorry. I meant to say it's not the truth."

Joan's brows tented in the middle. "When the villages are empty, you can bet they'll come back and steal everything that isn't nailed down. And then they'll say it was the thieves or something."

"Lovely!" Eleanor said, dripping with sarcasm. "They move us out because of thieves, but they're the ones who are doing the thieving!"

The breath flew out of Robyn. All that adventure and excitement and fear . . . all that effort of getting back their stolen food and clothing and tools . . . only to have them stolen again. There was absolutely no doubt in her mind they'd take everything they could from the village as sure as chickens laid eggs.

At least their winter wheat was safely in the ground.

The others kept talking and complaining for a while, which gave Robyn time to think. In a clear, firm voice, she said, "Everyone, be quiet, I know what to do." To her surprise, her mother,

Joan and Marion all stopped talking and turned to her. What power!

"Joan, I'm sorry about this but we need to take everything of value that's left in the cottages and pile them into the tower."

Instead of questioning Robyn, Joan immediately nodded and said, "Good idea!" Then she set off towards her cottage to raid her parents' belongings.

Eleanor looked at her expectantly, awaiting orders. If Robyn weren't careful, this power trip would give her delusions of grandeur.

"Mother, take Shadow down to the river, and keep her out the way. We can't risk them recognizing her. See if you can find the chickens while you're down there."

"Will do. Come on girl," Eleanor clicked her tongue and guided Shadow gently by the neck, leading her away from the village.

"What do you need from me?" Marion asked.

A lump formed in Robyn's throat. Checking left and right to make sure the others were out of the way, Robyn kept her voice low and said, "I need you to tell me what this says."

She steeled herself for laughter. Derision. Confusion. None of it came. Marion merely nodded and read the parchment, his voice low so they wouldn't be overheard. Shame flooded her. He must have known all along that she couldn't read.

Marion didn't boast either. The very least he could do was look smug; that way she could get properly cross with him. But no, he was all understanding and compassion. Damn him.

The moment he finished reading, he rolled the parchment up and pointed to an empty cottage. "I'll raid that one."

"Good, I'll climb the tower and see if they're coming."

"Gotcha." And off he raced.

Back up the tower Robyn charged, her heart pumping fast with excitement and fear. She scrambled up the flights of ladders and trapdoors until she was high above the world, looking back towards Loxley.

With shoulders hitching towards her ears, Robyn tried to stay calm. There was no sign of the Sheriff's men, yet.

Cool autumn winds teased her neck as she scanned the neighbourhood. She was grateful for the season of trees with bare branches. If it were summer, the leaves would be so thick and lush she wouldn't be able to see the road.

Below, Joan and Marion raided each house and brought clothes, pots and even three-legged stools out.

Joan tossed the pieces up, and one by one Robyn caught them and shoved them over by the wall. Speed was the essence, not neatness. Meanwhile, Marion raided the two remaining cottages, his arms overflowing.

Get it done, then get safe. "Is that all of them?" Robyn called out as she caught a clay pot and placed it to the side.

"Can't see anything else," Marion said.

"That's why we're called Littleton," Joan said, adding a grin.

Marion pointed over his shoulder. "What about the cottages back that way, around the bend?"

"No, too far away, they could be here any moment," Robyn said as she caught a folded sheepskin. "Climb up to the top and keep watch for us."

Before Marion could place a hand on the ladder, Joan threw up an axe.

Robyn yelped as the weapon made swoosh going past her head.

Clanggggg! The axe took a chunk out of the wall.

Robyn's heart nearly scrambled out her throat in fear.

"Watchit!" Robyn and Marion yelled at the same time.

"Sorry!" Joan said. "I did throw it handle first."

"Are you all right?" Marion asked as he clambered up.

"Yeah, course."

"Better we have the axes than they do," Joan said from below. "Keep back, I'm throwing another one up now."

Robyn kept well back as the second axe sailed past.

Taking a quick stock take, they had plenty of pots and cloths and small farming tools. But nothing to eat. Grabbing an earthenware jug, Robyn tossed it down to Joan, who caught it in her strong hands. "Fill this up from the river, then bring mother back here as fast as you can. If the Sheriff's men get here before then, get out of town, all right?"

Joan gave Robyn a wink and a salute, "I'll leave you two alone if that's what you mean."

Heat tore through her. "Hey, what?" Robyn called after Joan, but the rude girl only waved as she jogged away.

Robyn made ready to climb down the ladder and set Joan straight when Marion called out from above, "They're coming!"

CHAPTER 4

*H*eart racing faster than galloping horses, Robyn hauled up the ladder below her to cut off access. At least now they were safe from the Sheriff's men climbing after them.

"Good thinking," Marion said as he came down to help.

"But now Joan won't be able to get up."

Marion scratched his head for a moment. "She and Mother Eleanor are smart. They'll stay by the river. Let's get the next ladder up as well." Marion said.

It was exhausting work. Robyn welcomed the burn in her muscles, it meant she was too busy to acknowledge the guilt swirling through her. Guilt for not thinking properly when the taxmen had first come to Loxley. For not thinking of some other way to save their grain without getting everybody into trouble. Every trapdoor they closed made the inside of the tower that much darker. Dust scratched her throat and nose. As they scrambled out the last hatch to the top of the tower, the air had never smelled so crisp.

Marion pulled a loose stone block from the top of the battlements and carried it over to the trap door, jamming it shut from above.

"Nice one, muscles," Robyn said.

"Thanks Robbie." Marion shrugged away the compliment.

Peeking from behind the walls, they saw the Sheriff's men. Their horses leading a single carriage clip-clopped into Littleton. They were wearing ordinary clothes and coats. Some had shiny long boots with buckles that gleamed in the sun, others had laced-up shoes. She hadn't seen such a mismatched team since her father had marched off with the village men to join the crusade.

The only motif signifying their team status was a brown armband with a sheaf of wheat on it; the herald of Sheffield. Robyn scratched her brain and concluded their liege lord in Sheffield had to know about everything that had happened in Loxley–but only from the taxmen's point of view.

"All stop," the man in charge said.

Robyn whispered to Marion, "It's the same man from the yesterday."

"Come back to finish the job," Marion said with an equally low tone.

In silence, they watched as the men creaked and groaned from their positions on the horses and carriage. They looked sore and tired, moving stiffly. Robyn sent up a silent prayer of thanks for Joan giving them so many bruises the evening before.

The men shucked their riding gloves off and sorted themselves out at a leisurely pace.

Horror dawned on Robyn. "They're not here to steal, they're here to settle in." Maybe that's why Littleton was empty when they'd arrived? "Perhaps last night . . ." worry spiked Robyn afresh. After she and Joan had attacked them on the King's Road, the men must have been furious. Had they taken their anger out on the people of Littleton?

No, wait. When she'd found Joan by the river, she'd said they'd already been raided. Then again, what if the Sheriff's mob had gone back through Littleton after the attack and made things worse?

Marion scrunched his face up. "Littleton's so small. Why wouldn't they stay in Loxley? Our village is heaps better."

"The great Loxley-Littleton rivalry."

A whiff of smoke carried on the wind. Sniffing Robyn said, "Do you smell that?"

"Have they lit a fire?"

Lighting a fire was a sure sign of settling in. Of keeping warm overnight, getting comfortable, drinking and telling stories.

Why couldn't they simply go away?

Robyn craned her neck and peered through the toothy square gaps of the battlement. It was hard to get a good look because she was trying desperately not to be seen from below. If she stuck her head out too far, the tax collectors would only have to look up and they'd see her.

"I can't see it, but the smell is getting stronger."

"God in Heaven. Look." Marion put his hand under Robyn's chin and tilted her face upwards so she could look in the right direction.

Fire.

Coming from Loxley.

Or, more accurately, the smoke of a fire, which puffed and grew in size like a thundercloud growing from the earth.

"I'm going to kill them." Robyn's hands clenched into fists.

"Get in line." Marion grabbed one of the ladders they'd hauled up, then kicked the rungs free. Then he grabbed one of the axes and began sharpening the rungs into fine dagger points.

Robyn joined him. Their furious whittling soon produced a short pile of pointy stakes.

"Mister Roger," somebody called out from below.

Robyn and Marion instantly stopped and craned their ears. So Roger was the man in charge, was he? She made a mental note to remember it.

"What is it?" Roger said.

"Someone's been here. There used to be a sheepskin in this cottage, now it's gone."

"Aww, do you need something soft for your bottom?" Roger said.

The air filled with raucous laughter, which quickly changed to coughing fits as the smoke from Loxley's fires carried in the wind and coated them.

The smoke stung Robyn's eyes. Marion too looked uncomfortable. The knowledge the men below were bearing the same pain gave her some satisfaction. Then the truth of the situation made her angry all over again. They were burning her village!

"I'll get you back, Roger," she vowed. "You won't even see it coming."

Eyes watering, Robyn and Marion held their hoods over their mouths and noses, filtering out the smoke.

How strange that now, of all times, Robyn should notice how long Marion's eyelashes were. Had they always been like that?

Below them, Roger's men approached the nearest cottage and yanked a broom's worth of thatching from the roof.

A sharp metallic scratching filled the air. Robyn craned her neck again to see Roger striking a blade against a flint. Sparks flew out and caught the top of the thatching, turning it into a fast-burning torch. They strolled from cottage to cottage setting the roofs on fire.

Fury made her react. "No!" she screamed, grabbing a sharpened stake and flinging it down on them. It glanced one man on the side of the head. Oh dear, it came perilously close to the horses. Must not hurt the horses!

"Ow! What?" The man grabbed his wounded skull and looked about.

Marion piled a fresh supply of stakes right near Robyn's throwing hand, then a moment later he too flung pointy bits of wood down on the interlopers.

"Take that!" Robyn screamed, then lapsed into a coughing fit.

"Mister Roger, we're under attack!" A man yelled,

"I can see that. Take cover!"

Instead of returning fire, the men ducked under the tower. Well, they wouldn't be able to climb up, because the ladders weren't there. And if they did manage to scramble to the top, she and Marion would be waiting for them.

Arm poised to fling another stake, Robyn waited for the men to move. And waited. And waited some more.

The ground was littered with pointy weapons, why weren't they throwing them back?

Suddenly the men ran out and grabbed the horses, then charged away, fleeing for their lives.

"And stay out!" Robyn screamed after them. Which also brought on a fresh coughing attack.

Marion had slumped down behind the battlement, breathing through his tunic. The smoke thickened. Flames burst through the top of the cottages, the dry thatching burning fast and free.

Dizzy with adrenaline and smoke inhalation, Robyn slumped down and covered her face.

"Well, they've cleared off. We should get down now."

An unearthly "*whoomp*" of flames sounded below them.

Directly below.

The air filled with strange new smells, like burning bread. But there was no bread here. Only . . . *uh-oh! The bags of flour.*

"They've set fire to the tower." Marion's Adam's apple bobbed out as he gulped. "We're trapped."

"We'll have to climb over the side, come on," she urged Marion, touching the stones to make sure they weren't too hot.

Marion slumped against the wall, his skin turning as grey as the air around them. "Robbie, I'm no good with heights."

If Marion couldn't deal with heights, they were in all sorts of trouble. They couldn't climb down the ladders; they'd whittled them away. Jumping from this height was out of the question. But maybe they could jump down through the trapdoor to the floor below, and then leap out the windows from there? That wasn't so high up, was it?

"Everything's going to be all right." It was vital to sound like she'd thought this through. "We don't have to climb down from all the way up here. We'll jump down to the floor below . . . and then crawl out the window. How does that sound?"

Marion nodded as sweat broke out over his forehead. It was getting so hot up here.

Flames punched a hole in the floor. Thick smoke belched out.

The rooms below would be fully engulfed. So much for getting to the lower floor, they'd be roasted in no time if they tried. There was no way out other than scrambling over the battlements and making their way down the outside of the walls.

Robyn grabbed him by the shoulders. "We're going to be fine," she lied. She had to say something to get him to move, because if they stayed here they were roasted meat. "The stones have big gaps between them for your hands and feet, it will be just like climbing a ladder."

He only gulped.

Confusion addled her mind. "Marion? You got yourself up here without any help."

His voice came out so softly. "Yes but, it was dark when we climbed up."

The fire devoured the floorboards. They had two options. Go over the top or die.

"Shut your eyes. Shut your eyes and do what I say." It was boiling hot. Singed aromas filled the air. "Don't look at the fire. Don't look down. Just listen to me, got that? Right, we're getting out of here."

If anything, the heavy smoke became their ally, as it was hard to see all the way to the ground below. Robyn helped Marion straddle the battlement, his legs dangling off the side as they nudged and budged themselves until they were hanging on, vertical to the wall.

"Keep listening to me, keep doing what I say," she said, between coughing fits.

With a pained voice Marion said, "You're loving this, aren't you."

"Oh yes." When all else failed, there was sarcasm.

Just as she'd described it, the stones really were set apart like rungs on a ladder. It was easy to find footholds and handgrips at regular intervals. "That's it, you're doing great. Now, move your right hand down here, and grab on to the top of this stone. That's it. Good. We're getting there."

Was it her imagination, or were the stones getting warmer? Now that they'd moved a couple of painful stone courses downwards, the smoke started to clear around them.

Yet it felt hotter.

Because the tower was acting like a chimney, sucking in air through the bottom and sending it racing up to the top. The middle floors were completely alight, conducting heat into the tower walls. Thank goodness they weren't still up on the top, they'd be dead by now. "You're doing it. We're both still alive, and we can tell Mother Eleanor and Joan all about it when we get down."

Mother and Joan? Robyn prayed they were waiting this out somewhere safe, somewhere down by the river.

"You're doing great. Keep listening to me," Robyn said, desperate not to utter an ominous, "don't look down".

Block by block, limb by wobbly limb, they descended. The stones felt hotter than ever, but there was no way to protect their skin. She pulled her tunic sleeve over her palm, but it made it harder to grip the bricks. They'd have blisters for sure, but they'd also have breath in their body and that was always a bonus.

"I can't do it," Marion said, every muscle shaking.

"Yes you can, you're nearly there."

Marion pressed his body into the stones as if he could merge with them.

Robyn opened her mouth and her mother came out. "Look at me Marion. Open your eyes and look at me."

It worked though, Marion did open his eyes.

Praise the saints!

"Here's the thing. You won't tell anyone I can't read, I won't tell anyone about this. Deal?"

A faint smile spread over his face. "Deal." It came out in a whisper.

"Left hand, move it down to the next block, got it? Good, now move your right leg, that way you're covering more space and spreading your weight out more evenly. Good. Now move your right hand, and then your left leg. Right?"

"You said left."

"Don't get smart." Relief flooded Robyn. Back-chatting had to be a good sign.

They were doing it. And the stones weren't as hot all of a sudden. They must be lower than she thought. Looking down at last, Robyn nearly laughed.

"We can jump from here," she said.

"What?"

"Look down."

With a gulp, Marion obeyed and looked down. Then he too

laughed with relief. They'd climbed all the way down between the arches and were only three stone courses above the ground.

Robyn let go of the wall and landed with a welcome thud on the ground. Marion landed a short while later, having jumped from the second course.

The village of Littleton flamed on around them.

The tower beside them reduced to a shell.

All the supplies they'd tried to save had been in that tower. Now they fell as ashes.

They were alive, but they had nothing.

"Water," Marion said, getting to his feet and holding his hand out to help Robyn up.

When they reached the river, Robyn slumped into it, covering her entire body with coldness. What sweet relief it was to cool her burned palms and baked body in the water.

"Robyn! Marion! Thank heavens you're all right!" Joan and Eleanor came running up to them and splashed into the edge of the river. Eleanor stopped at the banks. "Get out of there, you'll drown!" She ordered.

"It's only waist deep!" Robyn said.

"I don't care. Water is for cooking, not bathing," Eleanor said, reaching her hand out to her daughter. "Now get out."

"Mother Eleanor, this is probably the safest place to be," Marion said as he got to his feet. He was soaked from top to bottom. His long shirt clung to his body, highlighting the muscles and planes of his torso. "Littleton is on fire."

"We noticed," Joan said, then she winked at Marion and said, "You should stay wet."

Marion snorted as he pulled the soaking fabric away from his skin.

Heat raced up Robyn's face, so she splashed herself to hide her embarrassment. Did Marion know she was looking at him? Weighed down by her wet clothes, she dragged herself to the banks and looked at the desolation.

"Sorry Joan." Remorse churned her stomach. Here they were, surrounded by water, yet they had no way of dousing it on the fire to save the village. The wind gusted in the opposite direction, blowing smoke away from them. It afforded a great view of what remained of Littleton.

Precious little. The stone tower stood there like a chimney, but the cottages were nothing but smouldering timber and clay shells. Their thatched roofs, made from dried straw, had never stood a chance.

"Wait a minute," Robyn said as she sloshed her way to the river bank. "Is that another horse?"

"Oh, yes," Eleanor said, "She was already by the river when we got here. Very friendly. Won't leave Shadow's side."

Must have been the other one Robyn had let loose when she'd stolen Shadow. They'd lost a village but gained a horse.

Shivers took hold as the breeze rolled around her sodden clothes. "Right, let's dry out." Slosh, slosh, slosh, she walked towards the closest ruined cottage, holding her wet tunic over her nose to keep the smoke out of her lungs.

There was nothing left to salvage in the cottage. Sunlight streamed in where the roof should have been. The walls were still standing, but the wattle and daub mud had cracked from the heat. A radiant heat, which helped dry her out a little.

Everything not currently smoking had burned to black coals.

"Hey, it's not so bad," Joan said as she gave Robyn a hug.

Robyn snuggled in to the hug and returned it with equal sympathy and love, dreading to think what might be left of Loxley.

"We're alive, yeah? That's always a bonus," Joan said.

"Since you put it that way," Robyn said, surveying the destruction all around them.

"Let's check the well. My parents were always throwing things down there, whenever strangers came into town. Who knows," Joan added with a shrug, "We might find something useful."

Four humans and two horses peered into the well.

"Is there any water in it?" Marion asked.

Joan shrugged. "Doesn't need to be. The river's always reliable."

"I can't see the bottom though." Marion's knuckles whitened as he held on to the stones around the top of the well.

Robyn swallowed, recognising his fear. "I can climb down, but I don't know how I'll carry anything out."

"Smart thinking." Eleanor took off her apron and ripped it into strips, then tied each strip together to make a rope. "It won't be strong enough for you, but whatever you find you can tie at the end and we'll haul it up."

Robyn began to climb, feet first, down the well. The diameter was narrow enough for her to anchor her feet and hands either side to support her weight as she shuffled down. It became darker and darker, so she had to stop a while and let her eyes adjust.

Breathe, it's not scary, everything is OK.

Her breaths echoed off the stone walls. Her thighs cramped with effort and she wanted to jump the rest of the way, but she still couldn't see the bottom. If she let go of the walls, how far would she fall before she hit the floor?

And what would be on the floor to break her fall?

The answer came a minute later when her foot squelched into soft mud.

"I'm at the bottom," She called up to the faces looking down at her.

It stank something putrid down here, but she had a job to do so she felt her way about.

"I found a rope!" She called out.

A moment later, Mother Eleanor's torn fabric fluttered down. Robyn tied the rope to the end of it. At least now they had something stronger to haul things out of the well.

The climb down was tiring enough. The climb up would be a total cow.

Using her hands to see, Robyn found a small bucket. It was already tied to the end of the rope she'd found. Hugely convenient. Next her foot tripped over a piece of wood. *Shlucking* it out of the mud, she saw that the wood was bent in the shape of a bow. It still had the string attached, although it too was slimed in mud. The string broke the moment she tried to pluck it. Great.

She slotted the bow into the bucket and dropped to her knees, sloshing through the stinky gloop in the hope of finding more goodies. A few coins in the mud made the effort worthwhile.

By the saints! She found the motherlode. Wrapped in thick fabric was a quiver full of arrows.

She wiped her hands on her tunic and placed everything in the bucket. "Haul away!" she called up. They would find something to restring that bow. Maybe Shadow would donate some of her tail hairs?

While the three above pulled the bucket up, Robyn slip-slopped away, finding a hammer and a large knife in the ooze.

A gasp of relief leapt out. The knife was in a leather sheath, otherwise she might have sliced her fingers off.

The stench from the mud made her gag. The sooner she finished finding things, the sooner she could get out of here. Then head straight to the river for a wash.

"This is really disgusting," she called up.

"Doing great, darling," Eleanor called down.

"Keep looking." Joan added encouragement. "I'm sure there's more stuff."

Urgh. Slop, slap, slip, squelch, stink. Breathing through the mouth was the only way to cope. With no choice but to keep on searching, Robyn spread her hands wide. Sludge oozed through her fingers.

They touched something soft, wrapped around something hard. Robyn picked it up—it was heavy—and unwrapped the putrid leather.

All breathing stopped as she boggled at a lump of gold as big as a fist.

THE SMOKING RUINS of three peasant villages lay behind them as Roger of Doncaster and his men headed toward Sheffield after a successful few days' tax collecting.

The stress began to ease out of his shoulders. His carriage groaning with goods should satisfy Maudlin this time. Perhaps after that, she'd finally be done with him and he could return to his family in Doncaster. He hadn't seen them for four seasons.

"Whoa there," he pulled the reins and the carriage came to a stop.

"Why are we stopping?" One of the men called out. "Are there highwaymen?"

Highwaymen? Not such a bad idea. After all, how was Maudlin to know how much they'd collected? "We have risked our health and our souls, for little payment." He said to his rag-tag team. "We have collected above and beyond that required by Maudlin. Here is where we take our commission."

The men–he used the term loosely as some of them were barely old enough to grow whiskers–wore confused expressions. Roger sighed. Did he have to explain everything to these cloth-heads?

"I'm creating a back-up plan," Roger said. "We deposit items here, just as if we were depositing it in the holdfast in Sheffield. The next time Maudlin sends us on a mission, we come here, collect the items and take them back. No risk of attack or injury."

The men nodded and muttered their agreement.

Half an hour later, they'd stashed nearly one third of their "taxes", all the smaller more easily transported items at any rate, in a strongbox hidden in the shrubbery.

Roger looked at their efforts and was pleased. "Good work. Now, I need a volunteer to stay here and guard it."

At first, nobody wanted the job, until the smallest of his men wordlessly put his hand up.

"Yes, you'll do." Roger tossed him a loaf of bread they'd taken from the hamlet of Hillfoot. "Sleep tight, we'll be back later."

With a flick of the reigns, Roger was on his way to face Maudlin. For what he hoped would be the last time. He had to get back to Doncaster with fresh supplies before winter closed in.

When they arrived in Sheffield, Roger and his team spread the goods from one end of Maudlin's banquet room to the other. It gave the impression of an almighty haul. She'd have no idea there was more deposited in a hiding spot in the Shire Wood.

Tureens of soup and wooden trays piled with freshly baked bread sat on the long table. The men stood behind Roger, waiting for the go-ahead. Rumbles from their stomachs reverberated around the room as the men shifted their feet.

A slow clap sounded at the far end. Maudlin strolled in, a small black bird on her shoulder. "Nice work." She said, casting her gaze from one end to the other. "I'm sure The Earl of Derby, our Lord Sheriff of Nottingham, will be well-pleased. You may eat."

The men fell upon the food, ripping the warm bread into chunks and ladling soup into their bowls.

It was almost too good to be true. Roger bowed to Maudlin and made a small cough. "My Lady, there is, of course, the small matter of payment for our endeavours," he said, raising his eyes to hers to see if he'd pushed his luck too far.

"Of course. You have done well. You shall be paid by sundown. For now, you may eat with your men."

Forcing a smile back, Roger bowed again and took his seat with as much patience as his salivating mouth would allow. *Don't smile, whatever you do.* They'd gotten away with it. He'd tricked the witch and now he was helping himself to her food. And on top of all that, she'd pay him.

"It seems," Maudlin said, approaching the table. She had to raise her voice to be heard over the slurping of soup. "You are a man down."

Gulp. Roger looked at the table and noticed the empty seat. Of course, Maudlin would notice. She wasn't stupid.

"We were set upon, by more highwaymen," Roger said. "Unfortunately, we lost one of our team. We had to leave him where he fell, such a pity. But I shall personally return to retrieve his body."

"I see," Maudlin tilted her head. "The thieves are still at large?"

"No, my lady." Needing time to think, Roger dabbed at his mouth with his tunic sleeve. "We defeated them. In any case, there is no way they can attack the villages of Loxley, Littleton or Hillfoot again, as those villages are no longer there."

Maudlin's eyebrows creased together, "That explains the dozens of peasants arriving at the gatehouse earlier today."

Roger continued. "We had to burn the villages. In order to save them. Now they can never be attacked again and the thieves have lost their base."

Maudlin look a breath and smiled as she turned to the bird on her shoulder. "Did you hear that Rook? I used to think Roger was an idiot. But lo, even an idiot can be full of surprises." She turned again to the men snaffling food as if it were their last supper. "Eat up everyone. You've earned it."

The bread wedged in Roger's throat as he tried to swallow. Maudlin made him uneasy at the best of times. He might be a paranoid man by nature, but that didn't mean the witch wasn't out to get him.

MAUDLIN WATCHED the men greedily take her food as if it were their right. They were one down, and she knew exactly which one because she'd placed her in the group. Disguised as a boy, of course, and in those heavy tunics and shapeless clothes the journeymen wore, who would be able to tell? But still, if Ellen were dead, more deaths would follow, starting with Roger.

She left the men eating and marched to the top of her tower, eager to look west and see the smoky ruins of the villages for herself. Rook cawed on her shoulder as she reached the lookout. The strong wind brought the smell of ash and smoke towards her. Gazing west, smoke rose from Hillfoot's general direction. Two more plumes arose from villages further west.

Her fingers curled into fists at how stupid Roger had been. Burning the villages had done nothing but create a false economy. Now she had extra mouths to feed and no future source of income. The fields would lie fallow. Where would their food come from now?

Holding her arm outwards, Maudlin clicked her tongue and Rook obeyed her instruction to climb out on her limb.

"Find Ellen, my darling. Find her for me."

With a flap and a caw, Rook took wing, following the Kings Road towards Hillfoot, Littleton and Loxley, as the crow flies.

CHAPTER 5

*L*ong shadows fell over Loxley as Robin, Joan, Marion and Eleanor turned the final corner into town. At least the sun was nearly gone for the day, it meant Robyn wouldn't have to see how badly her home village had burned.

"First thing. Let's go to the forge," she said. A new idea had grown on the walk back, and maybe if she kept busy she wouldn't have time to dwell on the horrible guilt growing inside her. "That is, if the forge is still there."

"I reckon it will be," Marion said, "It's designed for burning things in it, not being burnt."

Every cottage that used to have a thatched roof no longer had one. The walls had held at least. Perhaps one day soon everyone could return and rebuild?

The horses sauntered about, sniffing out food.

"I'm off to see if there's anything we can salvage," Eleanor said.

Misery leached Robyn's bones to dust. She ached to lie down but she couldn't rest. The village was little more than piles of embers. And it was all her fault.

She couldn't stop thinking about the tax collectors, and what she could have done differently so that none of this would have happened. Her mother had told her to run, she could have run into the Shire Wood and hidden. Then she could have walked back into town with her bag of wheat and they would have been so thankful to have something to run through the mill and make bread.

And the village would still be whole.

"Everyone get shovels or spades or whatever we have so we can bring the hot coals to the forge. It will all help, right?" She said to Marion and Joan.

"Whatever you say, boss," Joan said. "By the way, why didn't the forge roof burn?"

"It's slate," Marion said. But instead of walking into the smithy, he walked over towards the well, grabbed the rope and hauled up a bucket that made metallic clunking noises, revealing his tool kit.

"That is pretty smart," Robyn admitted.

"Glad you noticed, Robbie," Marion said.

The air fled Robyn's lungs. It felt . . . weird and strange. For a moment she stood there saying nothing, her mind trying to work out the source of the strangeness. But there wasn't time for that luxury. She had bigger issues to deal with, including whether there was anything left of her village to salvage, and the really, really, *really* big issue of–

"Where is everyone?" Joan asked.

Sickness rose in Robyn as she took in her surroundings. Really took them in. Not merely burning embers and destroyed houses, but an eerily empty village. A day earlier, she and Joan had returned triumphant with their stolen belongings and food. Hailed as heroes.

"They're all gone," Marion spoke the words Robyn couldn't bring herself to say.

"What, everyone?" Joan turned to Marion, as if he were somehow responsible for this. "Those taxmen must have turned up as soon as our backs were turned."

A heavy sigh from Marion. "Pretty much. Roger and his men came in, nailed up the warning sign about outlaws in the Shire Wood, then rounded everyone up."

"The bastards." Anger and guilt warred with each other in Robyn.

"Where did they take them?" Joan asked.

Clever, sensible, smart Joan. This was the kind of question Robyn should be asking instead of stewing in her own bile. Littleton had suffered as much as Loxley. Joan had to be crazy with worry about her doddering parents, but she hadn't let it cloud her judgment.

Unlike Robyn.

Marion's broad shoulders slumped. "Sheffield."

"Yes, but . . . where in Sheffield? Are they relocating them or have they all been arrested and thrown in the dungeons? How many wagons did they have?" Robyn felt a spike of pride at being able to ask something sensible.

"Only one extra carriage. They loaded it with everything they stole back from us . . . and made everyone walk back to Sheffield ahead of it."

"And where were you all this time?" Joan asked.

"Steady on," Robyn said.

"No, she's right to be cross." Marion said. "I ran and hid. Then ripped the sign off when they weren't looking and ran to Littleton to find you."

"Wait a minute," Robyn's mind stopped spinning for long enough to make sense of all this. "They nail up a sign, knowing full well hardly anyone in the village can read."

"Except us, of course," Marion said.

Her heart skipped a beat, but she didn't think anyone noticed. "Of course, but . . . they pack the rest of us off, and leave a sign up in an empty village, which they then set fire to."

"They think we're blokes, remember?" Joan said with a wicked grin. "Everyone knows most girls can't read. But some men can. My dad can . . . a bit. So they put the sign up to let us know they're on to us. Figuring we'll have to come back at some point."

Again Joan had it all worked out. The girl may look a brute, but she had a fine mind.

"OK, so they're sending us a message. Let's send them one back," Robyn said. The words poured out of her before she could chicken out. "We take the fight to them. We take back what's ours."

"How?" Marion asked.

"I'll figure the details on the way. For now, let's salvage what we can from here, then we go to Sheffield."

A broad grin split Joan's face. "I like it."

"I don't," Marion said. "We should think this through some more. Have a more detailed plan."

Robyn threw her hands up in frustration. "I've already given us a plan. Sure as the sun comes up in the morning, Roger and his men will be back here, raiding the village and the Shire Wood looking for us. But they won't catch us napping, because we'll already be in Sheffield."

Marion scratched at his top lip, as if the few soft whiskers there itched him. Was this his way of trying to remind them he was the man of the village? That he should be in charge?

Robyn wasn't buying it. She had her blood up and her mind fixed. "They've taken everything from us, we have nothing left to lose."

IN HER HIDING place beside the King's Road, Ellen took a woollen blanket from the strong box and wrapped it around herself. No way could she set a fire for warmth; the light would provide a beacon for anyone else to find her here. She didn't mind the cold. She'd grown up in the valleys and dales and had spent many nights sleeping under the stars. Watching over sheep and making sure most of them got back to the village. She only ever took what she could eat, mind. Especially when one of the ewes had twins. Twins were bad luck, weren't they? They drained the mother of energy and took so much longer to grow. To be honest, she was doing the farmers a favour when she weeded out a spindly twin to feed her belly. Or the male lambs. After all, the males would only be sorted out later so they didn't cause trouble for the flock in the long run.

Shepherding was always good while it lasted and she could usually last in one place for a few months until the locals wised up to her and ran her out of their valley. Alas, she'd run out of so many valleys, moved on so many times she wasn't sure if she knew know how to get back. And to be honest, she didn't know if she really wanted to. It didn't rain here half as much as it had in the valleys. And she'd eaten enough lamb to last her a lifetime.

Maudlin was a cracking woman. What a day it had been when their paths had crossed. She and Maudlin could have been sisters they were so alike in the way they viewed the world.

She couldn't wait to tell Maudlin about Roger. He was hopeless, to be honest. Leaving the smallest of his team to look after . . . what had he called it? Their commission? There was no way one strong girl could defend it if a band of thieves really did show up. Still, if she stayed quiet and kept herself warm by means other than a fire, the chances of real thieves stumbling across her were slight.

Ellen rubbed the bruise on the back of her head from the right thwacking that giantess had given her. A giantess-pretending-to-be-a-strong-man-pretending-to-be-an-old-crone with a wayward nag.

Oh yes, she'd seen enough to know when someone else played dress-ups, because she'd been doing the same thing herself for years.

Now Ellen found herself guarding double-stolen goods, and Roger was a right twit to think he was going to keep any of it without Maudlin finding out.

To be honest, Maudlin would most likely take her commission before sending things on to the Sheriff. And he'd probably take his commission before sending anything on to Prince John, looking after the King's treasury.

Her eyes fully accustomed to the darkness, Ellen set about making a soft bed out of fallen leaves.

Oh lush, she thought, as she mushed herself into it.

Being left behind was a bonus. No more hard work or marching or raiding villages for her. A night under the stars in a bed of soft leaves. Not a worry in the world.

Not a worry, that was, until Roger came back. And then what?

Uh-oh. Ellen sprang out of her bed as fresh troubles swamped her.

Maudlin was bound to notice she was missing from Roger's gang. What kind of lie would Roger invent to explain her absence?

The easiest one would be to say they'd been attacked. Would

Roger come back tomorrow and make sure, in a very permanent way, that she could never tell Maudlin of his deception?

Roger might be stupid, yes, but he was also dangerous.

The smartest thing she could do now would be to grab what she could from the strong box and hit the road.

A familiar "caw, caw" filled the sky.

Wings flapped overhead and a jackdaw, as black as a moonless night, landed on her shoulder.

"Clever girl, Rook!" Relief flooded Ellen. She dove into the strongbox and took out a piece of leather. In the darkness, she hunted for anything that would make a mark. The dagger would do.

Now she wished she had lit a fire so she could see better, but it was too late for that. She'd use the dagger to write some kind of message in darkness and hope it wouldn't result in slicing her thumb off.

With the pointy end, she banged in two eyes and a curve underneath, like a smiling face. Then she sheathed her dagger, rolled up the leather and Rook took it in her talon.

"Fly back to Maudlin," She said.

Ears straining, Ellen heard Rook's wings flap away into the distance. The raven would be flying towards Sheffield. Which meant she had to go in the opposite direction. Because if she went the same way as the crow, there was every chance she could run into Roger again.

She stumbled and staggered over the uneven ground until she came to the dirt road. The moon tried its best to break through the clouds, but she'd have to make do with the watery light it offered.

Enough light to show she was still wearing her boy disguise of loose trousers and a tunic, instead of a long skirt. Back to the cache of goodies she scarpered, raiding the boxes for anything remotely girlish.

An apron would do.

Back on the King's Road, she set off at a jog, trying very hard not to make a noise just in case any of Roger's men were about. The road took her past the turnoff to Hillfoot and on to a badly singed Littleton. She recognized it from the stone tower they'd set fire to.

Strong tower, didn't even look damaged.

When she walked under the arches, she could see clear up to the mottled sky. Oh dear. Quite a bit of damage then.

"Hello, is anyone here?" May as well check.

Nobody responded.

Like a spider, Ellen took to the outside of the tower's stone wall and scrambled up. The battlements looked completely unsafe so she decided not to climb on to them, but while she was up here she gazed around as much as she could. There was a blazing light up ahead. Could it be the other village they'd set alight? Was it still burning?

Or was it a sign that some of the people had returned?

Desperate to find out, Ellen scrambled down the wall and headed off towards Loxley.

AN UNFAMILIAR VOICE called out in the Loxley air.

Robyn grabbed the hammer out of Marion's hand mid-swing and stomped out into the night. "Who's that! Show yourself!"

"Only me!" A girl called out.

"Who's 'Me'?"

"Me is Ellen from the Valley."

"What valley?"

The girl took a step closer, but was completely non-threatening about it, judging by the way she held her palms up in surrender.

"Sorry about that, you call them dales here. I'm not sure there's much difference, to be honest."

Robyn lowered the hammer. "You speak funny."

The stranger said, "Your accent's lush too."

"You finished with this?" Marion snatched his hammer back so he could return to work.

Seeing the girl meant no harm, and from the sounds of her accent she had to be a long way from home, Robyn extended her hand in friendship. "I'm Robyn, from Loxley. Or, what's left of it."

"It's lovely to meet you. But I won't lie to you Robyn, I'm starving. Is there anything to eat?"

Pointing towards the darkness beyond the village, Robyn asked, "How many more of your lot are out there?" It was so hard to place Ellen's sing-song voice. Was she all by herself or was she with a whole group of travelling people and they'd sent her to the village to make contact?

"No, love. It's just me."

"I found Bella," Mother Eleanor said as she walked the ruminant towards the warmth of the forge. "Oh hello there, I'm Eleanor."

She and Ellen introduced themselves, before Eleanor called out to Marion. "Got any pails or bowls I can use?"

Ellen piped up. "Does your cow need milking then? Let me help, now, I don't mind."

A quick hunt through the forge yielded nothing useable. Until with a sigh, Marion handed over his incomplete helmet.

"You'll have to hold it, it's not flat on the bottom so it will roll over." He said.

Robyn made what she hoped looked like a sympathetic face. "It's a really handsome bowl."

Marion shook his head and stomped back to the forge. Soon the familiar sounds of clanging and banging rang out. Louder than normal. Taking his frustrations out on the anvil.

Ellen and Mother Eleanor set to milking the cow. One holding the bowl and the other milking. It wasn't a large bowl, so it filled quickly. They passed it around so everyone could have a drink before milking Bella some more.

"That's so warm and lush," Ellen said. "Thank you Bella, you are a truly beautiful cow." To make the night even more bizarre, the girl started singing.

How lovely a creature is the cow
  Far kinder than a goat or sow
  When the milking is done
  She's up with the sun
  And is ready to pull the plough . . .

"Can't say I've heard that song before," Eleanor said.

"Made it up just now this minute," Ellen beamed.

"Where are you from, exactly?" Robyn asked again.

It was hard to tell in the darkness, but she could have sworn she saw Ellen take a gulp at the question. Maybe a bit of milk went down the wrong way.

"I'm travelling mostly, to be honest. I lived in Blaenafon for a while, but most of the time we called it "The Valleys". Although now I think of it, Blaenafon was up on a hill. So that doesn't make any sense now, does it? But everyone knew it as "The Valleys" so that's what we called it. We mined coal from the ground and sold it to other towns. It's world famous that coal. Maybe the coal in your forge could be from us."

A twitchy squint made Robyn's eyes narrow. "The coal in Marion's forge is from what's left of the village."

"Oh, I am sorry about that," Ellen said, then covered her hand over her mouth. All too soon she took it away again. "Pay no mind to me, I won't lie to you, I do run off at the mouth."

Understatement.

"Where's Joan?" Robyn asked, looking around. "It's not like her to pass up a drink."

"Coming," said a voice from far off. "Just hitching up the wagon."

"We have a wagon?" That was news to Robyn.

Joan reached Robyn, bringing her beaming smile and a wagon with the horses behind her. "The Sheriff's men burnt the top off the carriage, so now it's a wagon."

"Why would they burn the top off their own . . . oh, they didn't know it was theirs, did they?" Madge had instructed the village children well, judging by the look of it now.

Joan beamed. "Now we can ride to Sheffield instead of walk."

"Mother's milking the cow. Help yourself while it's warm."

"Hello, who's this?" Joan said as she accepted the bowl of milk

–

– which Ellen dropped as she took a sudden step back.

"Oh, I'm so clumsy! I'm so sorry!" Using the cow as a shield, Ellen muttered about getting her another drink.

"This is Ellen a'Dale," Mother Eleanor said by way of explanation. "She's wandered in from the valleys."

ELLEN COULDN'T STAND clumsy behaviour in other people, yet that's exactly what she'd become at the sight of the girl giant. It had to be the same one who'd handed them their backsides on the King's Road. And now she was right here! Which meant any of the others in the village could be her accomplice. Would the giant recognize her? Please no, that would ruin everything.

It was dusk when they'd met on the road, and, praise the saints, it was pretty dark now. And she'd been disguised as a man at the time to blend in with the rest of Roger's men. Well, they had all been dressed as men, hadn't they? Still, there was no mistaking this tall girl as the one who'd given her a right walloping.

Then again, perhaps Ellen wasn't the only one with bruises? No doubt the giant had lumps on her head from forgetting to duck under doorways.

Don't be stupid, you can't hide behind the cow forever. Hand the giant her milk and if she recognizes you, make a run for it. Holding a full bowl, she stood up carefully, holding back the trembles as she handed it over. Not a flicker of recognition from the giant's face as she took the milk and drained it.

"Thank you very much, Bella," the giant said, then she handed the bowl back. "I'm Joan, by the way, nice to meet you Ellen. Are you here on your own?"

Yes and no. She had to think quickly. "I was with my family, we were going to Sheffield to trade, but the Sheriff's men stopped us on the road and we all had to run off in different directions."

"Him again," Joan said. "We'll have to clonk him harder next time we meet."

"You what?" Ellen asked, pretending not to know.

The girl called Robyn elbowed Joan in the ribs to hush her and said, "We're going to Sheffield ourselves, once Marion's finished up. You can ride with us if you like."

"I'll say 'yes' to that." Ellen was grateful for the warm milk in her belly, grateful they hadn't recognized her, and especially grateful for the offer of a ride back to Sheffield.

Going there alone would have been problematic; it was a long walk, and she might run into Roger.

Travelling with plenty of other girls and a bad-tempered blacksmith? It was the perfect cover.

Maudlin was going to be so proud of her when she turned Joan the giant in. So long as these villagers didn't work out who she was before then.

"Tie your frock," Mother Eleanor said, coming over to Ellen and looking at the state of her clothes. "My goodness but your skirt is simply hanging off you. Tie them up better so you don't get caught in anything."

"Yes, of course, thanks," Ellen took a step back and adjusted herself.

Eleanor tended the cow. "Joan dear, hand me that rope, we'll tie Bella to the back of the wagon and bring her too. And Robyn, for goodness sake, tie your frock as well. You can't go to Sheffield looking like that."

"Who cares what I look like?" Robyn said.

"I do, and so will the gatekeepers. You want to look like you belong, not like you're some desperate refugee whose village has burned down."

Ellen gulped at the mention of fire. She'd been one of the arsonists.

"Our village has burned down," Robyn stated the obvious.

"Let's not be telling them that either," Eleanor said.

Joan piped up. "We'll say we're traders on our way south to Nottingham."

Ellen stopped breathing. Joan had appropriated her own lie to suit them. Did that mean Joan didn't believe her after all?

Oh dear. Despite appearances, the lumbering giant had a brain as sharp as a pick.

Making a run for it back to the valleys suddenly felt like a really good idea.

Robyn kept up her chat with Joan the giant. "OK, just for the moment, let's say our plan is to pretend we're traders. What are we selling?" Robyn asked.

"Our spare horse?" Joan said.

"Not Shadow!" Robyn ran to the animal and hugged her neck.

Ellen tried very hard to stay out of it, but as she looked at the two horses Joan had hitched to the front of the wagon she knew exactly to whom they really belonged. These people were peasants; they were lucky to have a cow. Highly unlikely they'd have not merely one strong horse, but a 'spare' to sell as well. They'd stolen these fine beasts as sure as dirt was dirt.

The list of charges was piling up!

The lad Marion came out of the forge with several leather bags that made jingling noises as he walked. "We're not selling, we're buying." He tossed the leather bags to Joan, who deposited them onto the floor of the wagon.

"What are we buying?" Robyn asked.

"Whatever they're willing to sell," Marion said.

"What good will that do us?" Robyn asked.

"We're not really going to do that, that's just the story we'll tell them if they ask us."

"Is that your plan?" Robyn asked him.

"Got a better one?"

Ellen stifled a snicker. Oooh, that blacksmith really sounded cross. With any luck, they'd be far too busy fighting with each other on the way to Sheffield to even notice her.

"Fine then. Everyone in the wagon," Robyn said, climbing up and getting the hem of her skirt caught on the wheel.

"I told you to tie your frock," Eleanor said.

"Tie your frock, tie your frock," Robyn said.

Eleanor's hands turned to fists as she jammed them on her hips. "Don't mock me. Just tuck yourself in like a good girl."

"Tuck, tuck, there you go," Robyn said, tidying her skirts.

Ellen approached the wagon. A heaving shove came from behind as Joan "helped" her in.

"Sorry. Some days I don't know my own strength." The giant said.

With all five of them on board, the cow tied to the back and the two horses harnessed at the front, Ellen curled herself into a tidy ball as the wagon jolted forward.

What awaited them in Sheffield was anyone's guess.

CHAPTER 6

*F*or a girl who'd spent all her life in Loxley, with the occasional hunting foray into the Shire Wood and trade visits to Littleton for chickens, the journey to Sheffield was a huge adventure for Robyn. Shame it was at night, it was hard to make out any of the countryside she longed to see.

She thought about the adventures her father and the rest of the village men must be having as they took their crusade to the Holy Land. Would they be having battles on the roads? Would they be hiding in the forest? Did they even have the same sorts of forest trees in the Holy Land?

Oh dear. Her imagination started getting the better of her and she saw her father battling a fire-breathing dragon. Everyone knew there were no more heathen dragons in England, but what about other lands? They could have dragons that incinerated armies with one breath.

And burn the villages. Just as Roger and his men had done.

"Do you know which way you're going?" Marion asked as he sidled up to her on the driver's bench.

Irritation niggled Robyn. "Where else does this road go?"

"Don't get snappy with me. I'm just wondering if we should have waited until morning."

Why did he have to be so . . . *Marionish*? And what was with people using words like 'snappy'? A girl could be in a wonderful mood, but the minute someone accused her of being in a bad one, it became a self-fulfilling prophecy. The only way to calm down was to say nothing and wait for her breathing to return to normal.

Marion nudged her. "You're going silent on me now?"

Robyn kept her voice low so as not to alert anyone to her rapidly worsening humour. Make no mistake, if Marion kept up this niggling attitude, she'd be fair seething in no time. "You know full well if we waited till morning, Roger would come back."

A shrug from Marion. "Maybe he won't? Nothing left to take."

"Thanks for the reminder." Definitely in a foul mood now.

If not for the job of holding the reins, Robyn would have crossed her arms over her chest and turned away from him. As it was, she had to keep steering the horses. Straight if possible.

The clip-clopping horse and cow hooves provided noise, but not enough to fill the uneasy silence growing between them.

Why did things have to be so awkward between them all of a sudden? They'd always been friends and mucked about together all the time. But lately things were . . . different.

On they went, the cloudy sky providing a few glimpses of the moon to guide the way to Sheffield. The cold night air swirled around her neck, so she pulled her hood tightly over her head.

"It's not your fault, you know." Marion said at last.

"I never even thought that." Robyn sounded far too defensive to her own ears. Her guilty conscience told her if she'd not annoyed the tax collectors so much, Roger wouldn't have retaliated so thoroughly.

"No need to get defensive. Do you want me to take the reins for a while? Have a rest for a bit?"

"I don't need a rest. I'm fine."

Marion yawned. Damn him, she caught the yawns faster than the pox and she started yawning too.

"Not tired, eh?" Marion said, then gave his top lip another scratch.

Just a nod. If she opened her mouth to speak she'd yawn again.

She could have sworn Marion was laughing as he too pulled his hood up. He turned away, probably hiding another yawn. After a while, he asked, "Do you have a plan for what we're going to do once we get to Sheffield?"

Not really, but she didn't dare let on. "I've got it all under control."

"Yeah?"

"Course I have," she bragged.

"Fine by me."

Using her 'I'm in charge' voice, she said, "We'll be there soon."

"How do you know? You've never been?"

They had to be close because the horses were tugging that bit more on their harnesses, as if they knew the road.

"There," Robyn pointed ahead. In the distance, they could see light spilling over the tops of a high wall. It had to be the battlements around Sheffield Castle.

"What are we going to say when we get there?" Marion asked. "I'm sorry to carp on, but we do need a plan."

"I'll think of something." If he said that 'P' word one more time.

Marion turned to head back into the wagon tray, parting with, "Whatever you say, boss."

Boss? The word scratched at her conscience. Being the boss meant she had to be responsible for everyone.

Since when had that happened? Surely the adult was responsible?

That same adult–her mother–who'd been the one to bundle up the bag of wheat and told her to run. Yeah, that had turned out to be a wonderful plan. *Think, girl, think.* Marion's idea of being traders simply didn't ring true. Firstly, they looked nothing like traders, what with the soot all over their faces and hair reeking of smoke.

Secondly, they had nothing to trade. They had plenty of coin, but they looked so poor people would assume they'd stolen it.

The horses pulled them faster towards the watch house by the castle gates. There wasn't time to call Marion back to the driver's bench to make new plans. She had to improvise something.

She yanked out a nose hair to set her eyes watering.

Nothing for a second, then a delayed pain that really hurt!

So *much*!

Tears leapt from her eyes and her nose ran instantly.

Memories crashed through. Years ago she'd pulled out one of her father's nose hairs while he was sleeping. The carry-on that had erupted! Now that she'd done it to herself, she understood her father's yowls of pain. Tears flowed like creeks down her face. She wiped her nose on her tunic sleeve.

"Stop there," one of the guards said. A young guard from the sounds of it. His voice cracked in the middle of saying, "State your business."

"We seek sanctuary," Robyn said, "Our village was set upon by outlaws and we have fled. Please let us in."

"Outlaws? Where?" That was the other guard. He didn't come up to the child-guard's shoulder. One of his eyes looked . . . nasty. The light from his torch showed he was an old man who should be regular height, except for the curve clenching his back.

One too young, the other too twisted to join the war. They'd been left behind to watch the gates. Robyn reckoned she could take them both without breaking a sweat. But she had to play the weeping girly-girl so as not to raise suspicion.

"Outlaws have raided our villages and forced us to flee," she said. "We are all that is left."

"Are they in pursuit?" The child-guard said.

"No, but we have nowhere else to go, and as Sheffield is our Liege Lord, we have come here for protection."

"They could be following you." The child again.

"What village are you from?" The crippled guard asked.

Brain stalling for answers, Robyn wasn't sure if she should say Loxley or not. Roger's men might be waiting for them. "Riverton." Not exactly a lie. They did have a river flowing nearby. "Sheffield owes a duty of care to his peasants, he must take us in."

The young guard spoke "Well he's not here. He—"

"—Times have changed." The twisted man interrupted. "Camp out here and wait till the morning."

The cogs in Robyn's mind creaked and groaned. "We can't. The thieves took everything. We barely escaped with the clothes on our back and—"

The twisted guard blocked them. "–With fine horses, a wagon and a cow?"

Damn!

Desperation crept in. "We'll pay you." Robyn reached for Marion's bag and pulled out one of the golden coins. Not quietly enough.

"Sounds like you have plenty more." The old guard said as he lunged for the bag.

"No!" Marion sprang from the back of the wagon and thumped the old man on the shoulders.

"You're the outlaws!" The child-guard grabbed at Shadow's harness to stop them turning back.

The cripple recovered and lunged for the money. For an invalid, he sure was agile.

"No!" Robyn yelled.

Suddenly the wagon swayed and tipped. "Joan smash!"

The giant leapt out of the wagon.

"No Joan!" Marion cried out.

Clonk!

Too late.

The old man fell in a crumpled heap. The child-guard let go of the horse's harness and dashed towards a rope hanging from a bell-tower. One ring and that bell would alert everyone inside the walls to the troubles outside.

Robyn pounced on him, making sure he didn't reach that rope.

He covered his hands over his face and muffled, "Please don't hurt me."

"Joan smash?"

It took all Robyn's strength not to laugh. "No more smash," she said.

"But Joan want to smash!"

Beneath her, the boy trembled. Robyn shared his misery. "We don't want to hurt you. OK? So here's how we're going to play it. You're going to open the gates and let us in. And we'll give you a shiny coin to give to your ailing mother."

"How'd'you know she was sick?"

"Because you're doing a dangerous job for a little boy. Now stop crying and . . . oh Joan look at that, his face has gone scarlet."

"Is he all right?" Mother Eleanor asked from the back of the wagon.

"I'm allergic to horses." He confessed.

"What does allergic mean?" Robyn asked.

"Is that even a word?" Joan asked.

"It means they make me sick. And itchy," he said, rubbing his face.

"Oh you poor thing." Robyn helped him back on his feet. "Can you see your way to the gate? I'll give you a hand. Stop rubbing your eyes, it will only make it worse." *My goodness, I'm sounding just like Mother!*

"You are the outlaws, aren't you?" He asked, his voice no longer cracking with nerves.

"We're not. But our village is now a burning ruin after the Sheriff's tax collectors set fire to it. We really don't have anywhere else to go." Adding a shrug felt natural to Robyn, as if she and this boy could both stop playing their roles and be themselves.

"Are you sure you want to go in?" He asked. "You might be safer out here in the long run."

Robyn gave the boy two golden coins instead of the one she'd promised him. "The rest of our village is behind the gates. We have to find them. Make sure they're all right."

"Will he be all right?" The red-faced boy asked, pointing to the crumpled shape of the old guard on the ground.

Stepping over to him, Robyn gave the crooked man a gentle shove on the shoulder with her boot, but heard nothing. Oh dear. She bent low and - relief! - felt his slow breath on her cheek. Thank goodness he was still breathing! "He'll be fine, but he'll have an aching head when he wakes up." Then she turned to the boy. "Sorry about the allergy."

He sniffed, "Once the horses are gone it will clear up."

"I feel bad about this. My name's Robyn." She extended her hand in a show of friendship.

The boy shook it. "Wilfred. Everyone calls me Will."

Marion led the horses towards the gate as Wilfred lifted the heavy timber from the latch.

The heavy gate, however, didn't open. Marion leant a hand, then Robyn too. "Joan," she called out, "care to help?"

"Can I do anything lovvie?" Mother asked. Not that she'd climbed out of the wagon the entire time.

"Is it locked from the other side?" Robyn asked as she heaved and hauled against the gate.

"Might be," Wilfred said.

"You could come and help," Robyn shot back to her mother. "Wake up Ellen too. Free ride's over."

They pressed with all their weight against the heavy wood. It budged, it sprang back; they leaned harder again and it sprang back even more.

One last push—*yerk!*—the gates gave in and Robyn, Wilfred, Marion and Joan fell forward with a yelp into the mud.

"Enjoy your trip?" A mocking voice said.

Robyn looked up to find herself staring into the smirking face of Roger of Doncaster.

Robyn *shlucked* herself out of the oozy mud to face her nemesis.

"Get out of my way, peasant!" Roger shouted.

Which only served to boggle Robyn all the more. And of course, as she stood there boggling, she kept not moving and Roger became angrier.

Did he not recognize her? Not even a little bit?

"Idiot!" He shoved her in the shoulder and sent her sprawling into Joan and Marion, knocking them all over like dominoes.

Joan whispered in her ear, "Want me to smash him?"

"Wait–"

Mother Eleanor piped up, "Don't you push my daughter around!"

"Do not stand in the way of the Sheriff of Nottingham's business!" Roger said as he stormed past. A straggly gang of young men followed him, ignoring Eleanor's protests.

Bella made a bovine moan as they jolted her on their way out. Poor Bella. Why were people so horrible to cows? They gave so much milk and asked so little in return.

As soon as Roger'd team were gone, Robyn scraped off the biggest clods of mud from her tunic and skirts and went to the cow's aid.

That's when she noticed the moving lump of sheepskin in the back of the wagon. "You can come out now Ellen, they're long gone."

Ellen peeked out from underneath. "I wasn't hiding. Honestly. But I thought it would be best if I stayed out of the way."

"Of course you did."

With Roger and his men gone, Wilfred guided them through the gates and inside the protective walls of Sheffield Castle. It was dark and difficult to see their way clear. The larger buildings leaked golden light from open fires burning in the hearths inside.

Wilfred pointed and said, "*The Goose and Bridle* is the best place to get lodgings. Best place for vittles is *The Unicorn*."

"Thanks for the tip," Robyn reached into her pocket and drew out another coin.

Wilfred snatched for it, but Robyn held back, a better idea forming. "You get this when we're on the way out. It will work out best for everyone if we're not harassed."

They stared at each other in understanding. Wilfred rubbed his sore eyes again and said, "Sounds to me like you might need a guide. Y'know, to make sure you stay out of trouble and don't get harassed."

Robyn smiled. "And what about your job as a gate keeper?"

Wilfred shrugged. "Godwin will wake up eventually. And you pay better."

"Godwin's the other guard?"

He nodded.

Robyn chuckled and said, "OK then."

"Let's get these horses in for the night." Wilfred said as he scratched his eyebrows.

"I don't like this," Marion whispered to Robyn as Wilfred lead the horses into the barn behind *The Goose and Bridle*. "How do we know he's not leading us into a trap. Or trying to steal the horses?"

A ferocious sneeze echoed through the barn.

With a tilt of her head, Robyn said, "I don't think he's the horse-stealing type."

Another sneeze, more violent than the first, ripped through the air.

"I don't know about you, but I'm ready for a kip," Eleanor said as she folded their belongings into her apron and tied the corners together into a makeshift hold-all.

"Will Bella be all right in here with the horses?" Ellen asked as she walked the reluctant cow towards the barn.

"They might let her in with us," Eleanor said, "Bring her over here and we'll find out."

Another ferocious sneeze barrelled out of the barn.

"He's going to blow his head off," Marion said. "I'll give him a hand."

Robyn rapped her knuckles on the back door of the inn. When the landlady opened it, she saw four women and a cow. "Right then, put the beast in the barn and we'll find a room for you."

"There's six of us," Robyn said, mentally adding Marion and Wilfred.

"And the cow stays with us as well," Eleanor said.

The landlady gave a haughty sniff and said, "If you want beasts under the same roof, you'll have to stay at *The Unicorn*."

"She stays with us at home," Eleanor protested.

"Mother, it's fine. Bella will be all right in the barn." Robyn didn't want to stand around arguing. It would draw too much attention.

At which point Marion and Wilfred came out of the barn. Wilfred's eyes had swollen into the shape of cracked eggs.

"Bella has to go in the barn too," Robyn said.

"I'll do it," Marion said, taking the cow's harness and leading her away.

The landlady didn't let them one step closer to the door. "We don't let anyone with pox stay here."

"It's allergies," Robyn said.

"Looks like the pox to me. He'll have to stay out in the barn." She said, crossing her spindly arms over her chest.

Wilfred sneezed so fiercely he stumbled.

"The pox! He's got the pox!" The landlady said. She took a step back and slammed the door in their faces.

"Want me to smash the door in?" Joan asked.

"Not this time. But thanks anyway. OK Will, if you can still see where you're going, take us to *The Unicorn*."

NO QUALMS from the landlady about the cow staying in their ground-floor room with them at *The Unicorn*. The dirt floor looked as even and dry as the one at home. The straw rushes had a fresh and welcoming wheaty aroma. There was a cot in the corner with sashes of hessian tied across the beams for a base. Eleanor put the sheepskin on it and pushed the frame into the corner so that whoever slept against the wall wouldn't fall out. She, Ellen and Joan lay down in it and declared it very comfortable.

Bella made herself immediately at home and slumped into another corner, chewing her cud.

Wilfred dipped a rag into the water bucket–Robyn hoped it was filled with water–and sloshed it onto his face. "Oh, that's better," he half-moaned as he sat on the floor and leaned against the wall.

"This is great, I don't know what you're worried about." Robyn rested against Bella's soft belly. The cow gave a moan of annoyance but didn't make any effort to throw Robyn away. She was so warm and soft, and the rise and fall of her ample stomach had a soothing effect. The familiar smells of the cow reminded her or home.

Which set off a pang of homesickness.

Would Loxley ever be the same again?

"Shove over," Marion said, moving in beside Robyn to share the warmth.

"Mmmmfff." Robyn wanted to object about the way Marion put his arm around her and snuggled in. But the cot bed in the corner was already full. Plus, the floor was hard and would grow colder as the night wore on. And for some reason having Marion's arm around her felt . . . kind of right.

And it would be the height of rudeness to keep the cow all to herself.

CHAPTER 7

*I*n the morning, Robyn's head thumped on the floor as Bella got to her feet. She picked straw from her hair and rubbed her eyes. The words "Where are we?" formed in her head just as Marion stretched and said, "Best sleep-out ever."

The others woke and commented about how rested they felt.

Wilfred, whose scarlet face had settled during the night to reveal a moderately handsome lad with a constellation of freckles over his cheeks and nose, looked at them all with a puzzled expression. "You're quite sure?"

A chorus of 'yeses' filled the room. Wilfred shrugged and shook his head in wonder.

"I'm starving." Robyn stretched again. "And I need the privies."

After they'd found the right places to relieve themselves, they made their way to the front room where the innkeeper presented them with warm bread and weak ale.

"You'll be having milk," Eleanor said as she gathered their empty tankards and dunked them in a bucket she'd carried in with her. "There's not as much today. All that walking must have dried Bella up. I've put her on the village green so she can get a good feed and plenty of rest to be back to her best."

"This bread is so soft," Robyn said, ripping a chunk off the loaf and dipping it in her milk. She had to lunge for it before the

71

sodden mush fell back in. Joan wasn't fast enough; her chunk dropped into her tankard with a messy plop.

Eleanor tried the bread on its own. "It's so tender you don't even need to dunk it. How do they do that?"

"This place is amazing, Will," Robyn said.

He boggled. "But we didn't even stay in a proper room, they put us in the shepherd's lodgings because of the cow."

"You mean they have rooms without any animals at all?" Robyn couldn't believe it when Will nodded. "Then how do they stay warm?"

Will shook his head. "You're weird."

"Would someone pass the honey please," Ellen said from her end of the table.

Robyn dunked her crust in the bowl before handing it over to Ellen, who proceeded to put a golden dollop into her milk.

"What a great idea," Joan said, taking the honey from Ellen and copying her.

Robyn achieved the same effect by eating her honeyed crust and then slurping milk at the same time, sloshing it around in her mouth.

The fresh bread and warm milk filled Robyn's belly, while the sweet honey sent sparks of energy through her. Buzzing filled her limbs and she had a sudden desire to climb a tree and swing from the branches.

"Right, what's our plan?" Marion said to Robyn as the last chunks of bread disappeared.

"We find our villagers and give them the . . ." Robyn dropped her voice low ". . . gold."

"Then what?" Marion asked.

Robyn felt her face crinkle in confusion. "Then they can buy enough stuff to go back and rebuild of course."

"Then what?"

Confusion irritated Robyn. "I don't know. I'm not in charge of them. They can do whatever they want. Stop criticizing me."

"I'm not having a go at you." Marion put his palms up in surrender. "I'm just concerned that if they go back and rebuild straight away, Roger and his lot could very easily turn up and steal things all over again."

The unspoken part of his sentence hung between them. Roger and his lot could set fire to everything all over again too.

At the end of the table, Ellen coughed her milk back. With all eyes on her, she dabbed a sleeve at her mouth and spluttered. "Sorry, a bit went down the wrong way."

Keeping her voice low, Robyn turned to Marion again. "You're saying we shouldn't give them . . ." dropping to a whisper "the gold."

"Of course we give them . . . *that*. But we've got to find them first, and when we do, maybe it's best if they stay here for a while."

"But this is Roger's base!" The words came out too loudly. People at a nearby table gave her strange looks. She lowered her voice again. "Wouldn't they want to get as far away from him as possible?"

"Yes but they'll be sitting ducks if they go back. There are hundreds of people here in Sheffield, they'll blend in with the crowd. And they can stay warm here through the winter."

"Then what's to become of Loxley?" And for a pitifully selfish moment, Robyn also wondered what would become of her. She wanted to go back home and make everything normal again. Well, it wouldn't be completely normal until her father came back, but she'd take what she could get for now.

"Loxley can wait until spring," Marion said. "It's not going anywhere."

"What about . . ." Robyn dug about in her mental basement, looking for reasons to return to Loxley and rebuild. "What about the crops we've worked so hard to get in the ground. Twice!"

"They'll either be there or they won't. Us returning to Loxley won't make them grow any faster."

Confusion swirled through Robyn as she ate the last of her bread. Surely once they found their villagers, they'd all want to go home? Why couldn't Marion accept that?

A new thought hit her in the belly. "You're not going back, are you? You want to join the Crusade."

"It's every man's duty to follow his King into battle."

"But your mother forbids it!"

"My mother isn't here."

"Yes she is . . . somewhere in Sheffield. I'm going to find her. And everyone else. And then we are all going home."

"I'LL STAY with Bella on the green," Eleanor said as they left *The Unicorn*.

"You could sell her milk while you're here," Ellen said. "Best drink I've ever had."

Eleanor's face lit up. "Good idea. I wonder if the inn will sell us some honey to go with it?"

At least her mother was happy, so that was one less person for Robyn to worry about. Still, it didn't sit right to leave Eleanor here in the village green, all alone with a valuable cow. "Ellen, stay here with Mother Eleanor and Bella, will you?"

"But, I want to come with you."

"I could stay," Joan suggested.

No, Joan would scare the customers. Anyway, they might need her later for smashing duties. Wilfred was their guide, so he couldn't stay behind. And Marion . . . well, he'd charge off and join the Crusade the moment her back was turned.

"How well do you know Sheffield?" Marion asked Ellen.

Which was the question Robyn was going to ask, she really was.

"Em. You've got a point there," Ellen said. "Not very well."

Mentally, Robyn waited for Ellen's usual 'to be honest' ending, but it didn't come.

"OK, that's settled. Ellen, it's best you stay here with Mother Eleanor and the cow. Will? Lead on."

In comparison to Littleton, Loxley had seemed a busy place. But now they were in Sheffield, Robyn realized how small her small home town had been. On this cool autumn morning, Sheffield positively heaved. There had to be two thousand people here at least.

How would they find their villagers in such a massive crowd?

"What's your plan?" Marion said as they began their walk down one of the bustling streets.

Sarcasm at the ready, Robyn said, "The plan is to wander around aimlessly until we're hungry and lost."

"You know what I mean."

Robyn walked faster, her hand over the purse of gold to stop it jingling. "I don't think it takes much planning to find the rest of Loxley, share the coins and get out of here."

"It's just that 'Get out of here' is hardly an exit strategy."

This time Robyn pulled up short.

"Don't roll your eyes at me," Marion said.

"I'm not ro–" Whoops; she was rolling her eyes. She focused every muscle in her face to make sure she didn't roll them again and said, "We're helping our villagers, yes? Then we rebuild. Is that enough of a plan for you?"

"It's a start but–"

Robyn didn't hear the rest of what Marion said as she stomped forward. The boy was driving her to distraction. He'd never been this bossy towards her before.

Their whole lives had been one season after another, one predictable event after another. Until Roger of Doncaster had come to their town, they'd left all the thinking and planning to the elders.

Now they were separated from the wiser heads of the village, they had to do all the thinking and forward planning themselves. It was exhausting.

Behind her, she heard the heavy footsteps that could only belong to Joan.

"Go easy on Marion, he's trying to help," she said.

"He's trying my patience," Robyn shot back.

"Yeah but it doesn't hurt to stop and think every now and again, he's only–"

"–We don't have time to stop and think!" Sick guilt lurched through Robyn as she heard how nasty she sounded to her friend. "I'm sorry. I really am. But we can't stay in Sheffield, and neither can the rest of Loxley. If we stay, Roger and his gang will return. It's only a matter of time before we cross paths again."

"But he's not looking for us, is he? He's looking for a band of men. That's why he pushed us out the way at the gate."

"We got lucky." Robyn kept up her punishing pace, her breath coming out as harshly as her words. All the while she kept looking at the faces in the street for someone familiar. "Roger didn't recognize us because he was in a hurry to leave."

Joan's heavy hand thumped down on Robyn's shoulder, bringing them both to a staggering halt. "And where do you think Roger was off to in such a rush?"

"I don't know and I don't care. Look, Joan, we don't have time to stand here arguing, we need to keep looking. Our people have to be here somewhere."

On they went, down the laneways between the higgle-piggle houses and animal pens, trying to find someone they knew.

In a petulant voice, Joan said, "I don't like arguing."

"Neither do I." Robyn felt awful about how this was turning out. "I am sorry. I really am. Anyway, we weren't arguing. We were only having a loud conversa–Madge? Is that you?"

The girl in question–Madge the Miller's daughter–was mucking out a sheep pen. She dropped her pitchfork at the sound of her name. A smile split her face. "Robyn! And Joan! And Marion! And . . . hello, new person!" At which point her smiling face turned bright red, almost as red as Wilfred's had been in reaction to being near a horse.

MADGE FILLED Robyn in on how everyone in the village had fared since their eviction from Loxley. In a word: miserably.

The sky above them looked like it was about to turn miserable as well. Thank goodness they had a sheep pen to huddle beneath.

"I am so glad to see you, I can't tell you how crazy things are," Madge babbled. "It's only me and Grannyma and Tuppence. We've eaten nought but turnips since we left Loxley, although we've given sheep milk to the babby. Not that Tuppence is a babby any more, have you seen the teeth on him? Milk won't be enough for him for much longer."

Guilt rained on Robyn like the drops falling from the sky. This morning they'd had the softest bread in the world, dipped in honey, to break their fast. As Robyn checked her pockets to see if she had any food to offer, Marion stepped forward and produced the end a loaf. Madge fell upon it as Grannyma came back from milking one of the ewes.

"You're supposed to be quiet!" She said to Madge. "I can hear you from the street."

Everyone hushed.

"That's better." Grannyma said. "We're trying to keep a low profile, obviously."

A sheep trotted over to see what they were eating. Robyn gave it a pat and it scarpered away. "Um, Grannyma Miller, whose animals are these?"

"No idea, Lovvie, but they couldn't very well milk themselves so we're helping out."

"What if the owners come back?"

"Then we'll have done them a favour. If sheep aren't milked on a regular basis, they stop producing."

Robyn boggled. "OK. And, um, where are you living?"

"Right here of course." Grannyma Miller looked at her like the chatelaine of a grand estate.

There wasn't much space for herself, Marion, Will and Joan to stay. Maybe they should take them back to *The Unicorn*?

"Where is everyone from Loxley?" Marion asked Grannyma.

Why hadn't Robyn thought of asking that?

Grannyma held her palms out to the side. "We're it, love. They took the rest."

"Have you seen anyone from Littleton?" Joan asked.

"No sweetie, I'm sorry, I haven't," Grannyma said.

More guilt weighed Robyn down. Nobody from Loxley or Littleton. Not good.

Grannyma continued. "Don't take it so poorly, you weren't to know. After they came to Loxley, they set us on the road and walked us here. Once we got through the gates, Madge and Tuppence and I snuck off and stayed here with the sheep to keep warm. We've tried to find out what happened to the rest and . . .

77

I'm sorry to bring bad news but I think they're all locked up in the dungeon."

Bile rose in Robyn. Before she could ask any more questions—as if her brain could work anyway—Grannyma Miller clasped Joan's hands.

"Oh sweetheart, your hands look awful. Come and rub them in the sheep's wool, the lanolin will fix them right up."

"Cheers for that," Joan said as she followed Grannyma's suggestion.

"Oh goodness, look at your poorly hands as well," Madge said to Wilfred. "Come with me, we'll have them all better in no time."

Utterly baffled, Robyn steadied her breath and tried to sort out what was going on. As far as she was concerned, everything had turned out about as badly as could be, and yet they were stopping everything to have manicures?

"Don't take this the wrong way, but I think we really need a plan this time," Marion said as he and Robyn mucked out the sheep pen together.

"Yes, yes." Each reminder of their situation added to the weight on her shoulders. They should be freeing their village people. Instead they were playing at shepherds.

Marion worked faster to get the job done. Perspiration made his shirt stick to his chest, which proved monumentally distracting.

"I'm not having a go at you," he said. "But we do need to work something out."

She couldn't be cross at him for stating the truth. And he'd said 'we', which made her feel like they were sharing the load. The gold in her leather pouch weighed almost as heavily as her burdens. "Part one of the plan, you carry this." She held it out to him.

"What am I going to do with it?"

"You're the one who says we should plan everything, so maybe you should be the one to carry it?"

Marion weighed it in his hand and was lost in thought for a moment. Then, he said, "Let's share it. That way, if one of us is caught or lost or we get split up or something, the whole purse isn't gone."

"That . . . makes a lot of sense," Robyn managed.

"You're welcome," he said, giving her a wink.

Robyn's stomach did a strange flip and her heart kicked like a freshly caught rabbit.

Meanwhile, Joan and Grannyma Miller fed the sheep and Madge stuck close to Wilfred, the two of them casting shy glances at each other, oblivious to the worries of the outside world. Why couldn't she and Marion be like that, instead of having to make plans and be responsible for everyone else?

They had a village elder here with them too, so why wasn't Grannyma Miller taking over the decision making?

A sense of vague disappointment with the world hung about Robyn like a hand-me-down coat.

"Robyn! Robyn, where are you!"

Hang on, that voice sounded like . . .

Ellen ran down the street, calling their names.

"Over here!" Marion called out.

"Oh, thank the angels I found you. They've arrested Mother Eleanor!"

Cold fear trembled through Robyn. "Where is she?"

"This way!" Ellen grabbed Robyn by the arm and they took off, running and stumbling down the street.

"Wait!" Marion called out behind them.

But Robyn had no time to argue the point with Marion. Her mother had been arrested! This was terrible!

Panting for breath, they skidded to a halt in the village green to find Bella standing there, munching away on the grass as if nothing had happened. OK, at least they hadn't harmed the cow.

"What happened?" Marion said as he pulled up beside them.

Ellen swallowed a few times and then reached for the milk bucket to quench her thirst.

"Where is she?" Robyn screamed at Ellen. Why was the girl stopping for a drink when her mother could be in danger?

Ellen put the bucket down and wiped her face. "They arrested her for selling milk without a permit. We have to go to Maudlin and pay bail money."

Before the words, "what's bail money?" could cross Robin's brain, Ellen was beckoning them to follow her towards the tower. No time to think, Robyn followed.

"Hang on a minute." Marion called out.

"There's no time!" Ellen said.

Robyn left Marion behind to keep pace with Ellen. As they reached a corner, Robyn slid sideways to catch a glimpse behind her. The crowd was too dense, she couldn't see Marion. Irritation nagged Robyn, knowing when Marion did catch up, he'd give a lecture about planning things first.

"Where is she?" Robyn now wished she'd glugged some of that milk as well, her mouth had turned as dry as summer dirt.

"Through here," Ellen said.

Blood pumping, Robyn blindly followed Ellen through a door, down a hall, then through another door until they burst into a massive banqueting hall.

Along one wall was a long dining table, enough to seat twenty people or more. Down one end was a stone fireplace, tall enough for a person to stand inside. It was fully lit, warming the length of the hall. Robyn could see no sign of her mother. Whipping her head around to the other end of the hall, she saw a magnificent woman dressed in darkly tanned animal skins, standing there with a jackdaw on her shoulder.

Who didn't seem the least bit surprised by two girls crashing into her hall.

Sickness roiled inside Robyn. Nothing about this felt right.

"Hail fellows well met," the woman said, striding forward. Her skirt hem touched the floor, giving her the appearance of gliding across the timber boards.

"It's the Lady Maudlin," Ellen said in a soft voice, "Bow to her."

Following Ellen's example, Robyn lowered her head.

Then Ellen took a step backwards, so Robyn did too.

"No, you're supposed to step forward." Ellen said.

"Oh." Robyn fixed her footing at the same time Maudlin

pinned her gaze on her. Cold sweat seeped through Robyn's skin as she took in the woman and the bird. There was something hauntingly horrible about the double-act, the bird as secure on her shoulder as a long-grafted tree branch.

"Come closer, there's nothing to fear," Maudlin said. The woman's eyes pierced Robyn just as surely as that jackdaw on her shoulder might stab a grub with its beak.

If free will played a part, Robyn would have bolted for the doors and made a dash for it. Her spellbound body moved forward as directed.

Lady Maudlin spoke with a clear voice, her tone sweet with an underlying cadence of malice. "You are here about the woman Eleanor, who sold wares without a permit?"

The words, "How did you know?" Formed in her mind, before the politeness filter came out of nowhere and had her responding with a "Yes."

"And you are her daughter?"

Again with the knowledge. Seriously, how did this woman know so much already? Or was she making really good guesses? Robyn turned to Ellen for some clues. Maybe Ellen had begged for Mother Eleanor's release already?

"It's complicated," Ellen said with a shrug.

Which gave Robyn precisely nothing more to go on. Only extra confusion. "Lady Maudlin," Robyn's voice came out scratchy and meek, because her body was about to fall in a heap of pathetic begging. At least she hadn't burst into tears. Yet. "I understand my Mother Eleanor has been arrested. I'm sure she meant absolutely no harm at all. We are newcomers to Sheffield and–"

"–I asked if you were her daughter. A simple 'yes' or 'no' is all I require."

"Yes." Robyn said, then nearly bit her tongue to stop it running on.

"And you have funds with which to bail her?"

"I beg yours?" Robyn turned again to Ellen to see if she could translate the lady's speech into plain English.

"Bail, my dear," Maudlin said ahead of Ellen saying anything.

The little crow fluffed her wings out on her shoulder, growing to double normal size.

"The gold," Ellen whispered.

"Oh yes. I have gold. Here," Robyn said, reaching for her purse. It didn't weigh as much as it should, on account of her halving it with Marion. What if she didn't have enough? "I'm ever so sorry. None of us have ever been in trouble before, so I have no idea how any of this works. How much do you need?"

"All of it." Maudlin said, unfurling her palm.

Acting before her brain had time to engage, Robyn held the purse and stepped closer to Maudlin. That's when the jackdaw took wing and flapped over, ripped the purse from Robyn's hand (making her yelp in shock) and flew back to her mistress.

Maudlin looked in the bag, jingled it, then looked not to Robyn, but to Ellen. "Is this all?"

"I'm sure there was mo—" Ellen sucked in her breath.

At which point Robyn's brain finally caught up to speed. She stared daggers at Ellen the betrayer. "You . . . *You*!"

Marion had tried to make her stop and think, but she'd been so worried about her mother she'd run blindly into a trap. Maudlin wasn't going to let her mother go. She probably didn't even have her! The woman was only interested in their money.

"Calm down Robyn or she'll arrest you too!" Ellen said.

The betrayal stung worse than a thorn in her shoe. They'd been so welcoming towards Ellen. Given her warm milk, a ride to Sheffield, a warm place to stay and bread with honey for breakfast. "What did we ever do to you?"

"This," Ellen lifted her tunic to show the purple-yellow bruises flourishing across her sides and back. "Your friend the giant walloped me a good one the other night on the King's Road."

"You were there?" Confusion curdled Robyn's stomach. "You burned our village!"

To her credit, Ellen looked ashamed. "I won't lie to you, I was in Roger's gang. But I never struck the flint or set fire to anything."

Robyn didn't want to hear excuses. Her hands clenched and unclenched, her body burned to punch a hole in something. Ellen's throat for starters.

But then she heard Marion's sensible voice in her head saying something like 'you need a plan'. Being angry and kicking and screaming, although immensely satisfying in the immediate sense, wouldn't get her anywhere.

No plans came to mind. Nothing sensible anyway. Maybe she should overturn the tables and throw furniture around the room. At least she'd feel better for having a tantrum.

Which would get her arrested no doubt, so it wasn't an option.

Whoa, maybe Marion's planning is having some kind of calming effect?

Ellen crossed the floor to be closer to Maudlin and the all-seeing bird. "You've done well," Maudlin said to Ellen. "For now."

For some reason, Ellen didn't look too happy with herself. Could it be regret Robyn read on her face?

It gave her hope and she once again reached for the security of sarcasm. "Yes, well done. I didn't see it coming." She gave a slow clap of applause.

The jarring percussion ricocheted off the walls. The jackdaw's feathers fluffed out as she shook herself. Who would have believed a little crow could look rattled?

"I didn't mean to hurt you, Robyn," Ellen said. "You're all such nice people, to be honest. Maudlin, why don't you let them go? You've got the gold now."

Maudlin made a wry grin and said to Ellen, "But you said there was more."

While they were distracted, Robyn took her chance to turn slowly around and take in as much detail of the room as she could. Marion's "make a plan" doctrine really was helping. Not that she'd tell him that, it would give him a big head.

How many windows? Were any of them open? The roaring fire could be useful, and the tools in the hearth. What else could she use for weapons? A broken chair leg? That could be good. And most importantly, where were the exits, and was anyone guarding them?

"I've got to hand it to you," Robyn made another loud clap. The jackdaw cawed with annoyance. Good. "You've got the rest of my villagers, you've got my mother and no doubt someone has already taken our cow from the green. But there's something you've overlooked. A few things really."

Maudlin smirked. "Oh?"

"You've overlooked the fact that I don't care."

"You're bluffing," Maudlin shot back.

"You've also overlooked that you're all the way over there, and I'm way over here." At which point Robyn shot off like a startled hare for the doors. She threw the timber slat out of its bolt and pushed the door free.

Not stopping, she darting through the alleyways. Just in case someone was following her, she ran in the opposite direction from the sheep pens where she hoped Madge, Grannyma, Wilfred and Joan would be waiting for her. Oh, and Marion.

Damn that Marion. She'd have to tell him what had happened, then endure a lecture about how foolish she'd been.

But she also knew a things Marion didn't know:

Ellen was working for Lady Maudlin.

And loud noises ruffled that hideous bird's feathers.

CHAPTER 8

W rung out from an evening spent explaining everything to Grannyma, Madge, Wilfred, Joan and Marion, Robyn yearned to curl up into a ball and hide from the world. But that was never going to be an option, not with the way everyone was looking at her.

Expecting answers.

Naturally, they'd taken the news of Eleanor's arrest badly. And Maudlin's play for their coins. And Ellen's betrayal.

And the unknown whereabouts of the cow–because Robyn had run the other way and didn't know if Bella was still on the green or not. It was a lot to process in one hit.

"We've been asking around," Madge volunteered, "There are so many new people in town, but none hailing from Loxley or Littleton. Maybe they are in the dungeons."

"Should we look for Bella?" Joan offered.

"Probably," Robyn said.

Marion said, "We should stick together. No more getting split up."

That was met with a round of assenting murmurs and nods.

Robyn moved things forward. "OK. What next?"

"No idea," Joan said.

"I'm not even sure where the dungeons are," Grannyma Miller said, feeding Tuppence some thin porridge.

"Me either," Madge and Wilfred shrugged in unison.

How much could they trust Wilfred? He'd only joined them the day before. He was sticking with them because they were paying him. He and Madge had taken a shine to each other, so perhaps he was one of them now? Or would he lure Madge away and their numbers would drop even more?

Hmmm. Madge hadn't seen Will in his full puffiness around horses, maybe the sight of his scarlet face would turn her off?

"The horses!" Robyn mentally slapped herself for being so dense.

"Oh yeah!" Marion said. "Good thinking."

Happiness beamed through Robyn like a rainbow after a shower. They'd left Shadow and the other mare in the stables, back at the first inn, *The Goose and Bridle*, not at *The Unicorn* where they'd stayed the night. Then she remembered something else. "Ellen knows where the horses are too. What if she and Maudlin are waiting for us?"

Marion made a thinking face for a while. "Got it. Ellen hasn't met Madge or Grannyma, so we send them."

Grannyma dropped her spoon, making Tuppence cry. "Count me out, I'm no horse thief!"

"No Grannyma, these are our horses," Robyn said.

Grannyma's voice slipped into 'scold' gear. "Don't tell big fibs. No matter how much you and Shadow might have bonded, she belongs to the Sheriff of Nottingham. They hang horse thieves, you know."

Darn those facts getting in the way of a good plan. Robyn sighed and mentally rubbed out the idea of taking Shadow back. "So, what are we going to do then?" she asked.

Marion put his warm arm around Robyn's shoulders and gave a comforting squeeze. Her need for reassurance took her by surprise and she leaned into him.

"We're all a bit strung out and tired. Why don't we have something to eat first and then we might be able to think straight." Marion said.

"Now that's a plan," Robyn said.

"Back to *The Unicorn*?" Wilfred asked.

Robyn jumped in. "What about *The Goose and Bridle*?"

"Where the horses are?" Marion raised one brow.

Robyn gulped. "Well, yes, but no, but . . . OK. Yes. I want to make sure Shadow is all right. I won't get us in trouble. And anyway, Ellen's just as likely to be looking for us at *The Unicorn* as the other inn." It made perfect sense to Robyn.

Grannyma huffed. "Don't blame me if we all end up in the dungeons."

THE ROWDY DIN at *The Goose and Bridle* made it hard to hear without shouting. On the plus side, it guaranteed nobody could overhear them unless they too shouted really, really loudly. And they weren't that silly.

Smoke belched from the open fire with each new log thrown on it. This was a crowded and popular inn, heaving with people and glowing with warmth. Exactly the place to be on a chilly autumn afternoon.

The landlord brought a pot of stew and a tankard for everyone at the table. Madge used one tankard as a ladle and served everybody. Robyn noticed how much extra Madge gave Wilfred.

The parts of the stew that weren't gristly were slimy, but Robyn didn't care. It was some kind of meat, probably rabbit or pigeon, along with grains of wheat and chunks of turnip. By the time she drained her tankard she had a full belly and felt warmed inside and out.

Across the other side of the room, a table of people started all shouting at once.

"Come on!"

"Wrong way!"

"Miserable little–"

"Move it!"

Curious, Robyn wandered over to check out why so many of them were shouting, transfixed by something on the tabletop. She had to stand on a chair to see what was going on, and found they were betting on snail races. Standing up high to get a better look meant she'd also raised herself closer to the ceiling, thick with fire smoke. A coughing fit made her stumble from the chair.

"Careful!" Marion was by her side, giving her soft pats on the back.

"I just need some fresh air," she said, slipping free and heading out the closest door.

Boosh! Robyn walked straight into the human wall of Roger of Doncaster.

Explosive curses leapt out of Robyn and Marion's mouths.

"Get out of my–" Roger started, then he grabbed Robyn by the shoulder, "–I know you!"

"No you don't!" Robyn said.

"Run!" Marion grabbed Robyn by the hand and charged away from the inn.

"Hold it!" Roger's vice-like hand clamped on her shoulder.

Robyn's joints strained from being pulled in opposite directions. "Ow! Let me go!"

"Not until I work out who you are," Roger said.

"I'm nobody!" she cried.

"Get your hands off her!" Marion yelled.

"Seize him!" Roger called out.

People appeared from nowhere and grabbed for Marion.

"Run!" Robyn begged him. One of them had to get away, to warn the others.

Darting between their assailants, Marion got away, shouting as he ran. "I'll come back!"

"Stop wriggling, little fish," Roger said, his breath sickly sweet.

Had he been in the inn at the same time? Robyn hadn't even noticed. Saints! She should have known he wouldn't be gone from Sheffield for long.

Rain fell over them in cold splats as she struggled.

He bellowed, "Tell me who you are?"

Robyn kicked him in the shins.

"Ow! You little–" Roger howled. "I'll have you for assaulting an officer of the King!"

Happy she'd landed a blow, Robyn said, "I'm not telling you anything."

"You will tell me or I'll throw you in the dungeons!"

Wait a minute, her mother could be in the dungeons. This could turn out to be a good thing. "Oh no! Please, sir, don't put me in the dungeons. I'll be ever so good."

Roger's voice cracked. "Really?"

"Course not." Robyn kneed him in the thigh.

Roger roared in frustration and wrenched her arm back, sending fresh pain through Robyn's shoulder and biceps. "I don't care who you are, you're going down!"

There was a scuffle and a dragging sensation as one of Roger's helpers grabbed her other arm and they dragged her away.

When they reached the dungeons, Roger shoved Robyn into the arms of the turnkey and said, "Lock her up for as long as you like."

"What are the charges?" The guard asked.

"Whatever you like," Roger said, then turned and stomped off.

It would have been the perfect plan if the dungeons, as Robyn had imagined them, had been one big room full of prisoners.

In reality they were a series of dark, dank and draughty cells.

The guard was a tall woman with an iron grip and a deep love of her profession.

"Please don't do this," Robyn said, only half acting. She figured most prisoners begged for freedom. But also? She didn't have to act too hard because the guard had a phenomenal grip on her upper arm. Robyn was beginning to lose sensation in her hand.

"It's my job," the guard said, giving Robyn a smile full of busted teeth.

The guard was such a giant, she reminded Robyn of Joan.

"But it wouldn't be your job, not normally. It's only the war that's taken most of the men away. You should be home in your village, making clothes and keeping the fires going and—"

"BORING!" The guard tightened her grip and Robyn nearly passed out from the pain. "In you get now."

The cell she threw Robyn in—then clanged the door shut and fastened the padlock—had nobody else in it. Judging from the echoing silence, the cell next door had to be empty too. Somewhere, she heard moaning. Somebody clanked a tankard on the bars.

"Hey Turnkey! Water."

"You should have collected it when it rained!" The woman yelled, then gave a wheezy laugh.

As Robyn rubbed the feeling back into her limp arm, she looked for a place to sit. The rubbing helped remind her she was still alive. Still OK. Still had friends on the outside who would bust her out.

Unfortunately, with only her deteriorating thoughts for company, she started to wish she'd taken Marion a little more seriously and made a better plan. A plan that involved all of them being on the outside of the dungeon for starters.

Rubbing her arm created enough noise to drown out the silence as she looked around her small cell for somewhere to sit.

Nothing.

Not even a large stone on the murky floor to use as a stool. After a few minutes she could feel her fingers and arm again, and her eyes adjusted to the gloom.

"Anyone here from Loxley?" She called out in hope of getting an answer. "Littleton? Anyone?"

Her voice bounced around the stone walls, mocking her.

From another cell, a croaky old man's voice said, "I'll be from anywhere you want, love."

Oh great. A comedian. "I'm looking for the people of Loxley and Littleton."

"There's me. And the voices; enough of them to fill a village."

If it didn't promise to hurt so much, she might bang her head against the wall in frustration. In between cackles of laughter from the vagrant, Robyn's ears strained for sounds of others. If there were more people down here, the air would feel different. It would smell like stale sweat and animal skins and wool. It would smell like bodies and mingled breaths. But the only smell Robyn could detect was her own body, and the remnants of whoever had been in here before. Using the corner to relieve themselves.

Let me get out of here before I have to use that.

The wall chilled her as she leaned against it. The pressure against her body offered little comfort. But soon, one wall wasn't enough security, so she squished herself into the corner–the opposite one to the open latrine–to feel the comforting pressure on two sides.

The floor was no doubt filthy, but it offered pressure from a third side and she took it. And lay there curled up for goodness knew how long, straining her ears for noises.

No noises.

Nothing.

The more nothing she heard, the more the tiny movements of her body sounded louder and more unbearable. Her pulse beating in her neck. The scrape of her tunic against her skin when she turned this way or that. Her fingers scratching her scalp whooshed in her ears like the bellows at Marion's forge. Nothing amplified every tiny something. When real noises eventually came her way, they nearly blew out her eardrums. Voices. Familiar and unwelcome, because they belonged to Maudlin and–ears straining–yes, it was Roger of Doncaster.

"Put it in this one." That voice belonged to Maudlin. Bossing people round.

"You're sure nobody saw us?" That was Roger.

It was impossible for Robyn not to hear their every word.

"Nobody saw us. But if it makes you feel any worse, the walls have ears so be quiet."

"How many people are in the cells? I sent a girl down here earlier."

"What for?" That was Maudlin's annoyed tone. Or, to put it another way, her default position.

"For her own good," Roger said with a wheeze, laughing at his own joke.

"Which means she can hear everything we say and do, so keep talking if you want to dig your own grave. I know the girl is listening. Aren't you?"

Cold chills radiated through Robyn. How could she ignore them when they were the only noise around?

"Aren't you?" Maudlin called out again.

A sigh of resignation from Robyn. "It's pretty hard not to."

"Show yourself," Maudlin said as she stood on the other side of the door and opened the inspection hatch.

"I won't look at either of you. Because I don't know who you are, which means I can't tell anyone what I've heard because I don't know who's doing the talking."

"Nice try," Maudlin said, "Take your hood off and show yourself."

Roger said, "Hood?"

The loony in the cell across the hall chose now of all times to call out, "Hood, Hood!"

"Let me see your horrible face so I may feed my nightmares," Maudlin said with a coldness that only added to Robyn's misery.

"Nightmares!" Came a cry from down the hall.

"OK then," Robyn walked over to the inspection hatch and pulled the hood off her head.

Maudlin cackled, "You! I should have known you'd end up here!"

Roger then took his turn looking at her. His jaw tightened but he said nothing.

"Come on, there's more to be done," Maudlin said.

The silence between Roger and Robyn spoke volumes. He'd have to know who she was now; the girl who'd attacked them that night on The King's Road.

GATES CLANGED and the door groaned open. Robyn woke to find the giant turnkey had come to her cell. "Aren't you a favourite?" the woman said, "You've got friends on the outside!"

Fat lot of good they were doing outsi– Whoa! Joan walked in and stood beside the turnkey. They could have been sisters. They were the same height and colouring, give or take a few layers of grime.

"This is wonderful!" Robyn said throwing herself at the prison guard, who made an 'oomph' noise from the impact.

"We've paid Maudlin the fees and you're free to go." Joan said.

Tears of gratitude bubbled from Robyn. Then reality poured in. "What, all of it?" They couldn't have used all their coins freeing her, had they? They'd have nothing left to give to their villagers.

Whenever they found them.

Joan said, "What are you waiting for, let's go."

"OK." Robyn boggled for a bit as she saw just how similar her friend and the turnkey were.

"Are you all right?" Joan asked.

"No," Robyn said, even while a smile spread over her face. "Oh wow, this is so great."

Joan's brows knitted together. So did the guard's. Their actions so similar Robyn wondered how the two of them couldn't see it.

"You weren't here long enough to go loopy . . ." Joan started.

Robyn kept right on smiling and said, "I'm fine, really. But Joan? Can't you see? I think this woman's your mother!"

A sledgehammer couldn't have knocked these two giants over, but Robyn's simple words made them stagger. Then they looked at each other as if for the first time.

The resemblance was uncanny.

How had they not seen it the moment they'd met? "You two need to find a water trough and have a look at your reflections."

"H-how old are you?" The turnkey asked, taking a step back to get a better look.

Joan looked puzzled. "This summer will be my seventeenth."

Robyn grabbed Joan by the elbow. "Come out into the light, you two, and you'll see what I mean."

All this time they'd left the cell door open, but she hadn't made a run for it.

"By the way, where's the rest of Loxley?"

"In the tower," The turnkey said, not doing a very good job of guarding anyone.

"My parents–" Joan began, then she teared up and dragged her dirty sleeve over her face, "They found me and called me Joan."

"Hello Joan." They stared at each other for a little while. "I'm Georgia."

So now the turnkey had a name. Fuelled with renewed hope, Robyn took this as a sign from the heavens that things would go their way. "Georgia, you're with us. Take us to the tower so we can free our people."

But the two giant women paid her no mind, both collapsing into tears and hugging one another. "I'm so sorry. I'm so sorry." Anything else Georgia said was smothered in a messy hug. The words probably didn't matter anyway. Just the sentiment, which was overflowing.

Robyn tugged on Joan. "Plenty more time for that later."

Joan pulled back and swiped a fresh streak across her face. "Stop bossing me around, Robyn. I've just found my mother. I mean, my other mother. I have a lot to unpack right now."

"Righto," Robyn shrugged and took to the corridor, looking for any other prisoners. But there was only one other.

"Leave me alone!" The weirdo in the other cell said.

"Don't you want to get out?" Robyn asked.

"Oh yes! Let me out." He changed his tune in a finger snap. "So much to do, so little time."

At which point Robyn figured she'd need the key, so she went back to the crying giants to ask them for–

"Isn't this lovely?"

There by the heavy doors stood Maudlin and on her shoulder the all-seeing jackdaw.

"Get back in your box!" Maudlin shouted as the jackdaw flew straight for Robyn's face.

Startled, Robyn ducked but the bird landed on her head, claws digging into her scalp. "Get! Get!" Her voice ricocheted off the walls, making her voice sharp, loud and panicky. Blindly she batted at the bird. It jabbed its beak at her hands in retaliation.

"Ow!"

"Stop it!" Joan shouted. Her voice did the rounds of the walls as well. "Georgia, do something."

"I can't!"

"Is someone going to let me out?" The prisoner down the hallway asked.

"Get this bird off me!" Robyn cried out.

"Please, Georgia?" Joan asked again.

"Get back in your cell and Rook will leave you alone," Maudlin's clipped tones jammed into Robyn's ears.

Anything to get the marauding claws out of her scalp. Robyn ran into her cell, but the bird refused to let go.

"Robyn get out of there!" Joan said. "Maudlin you thief! We've paid for her release, now let her go!"

"Hush!" Georgia warned.

"Get off!" Robyn's echoed. The raven's "caw, caw" noises bounced around the walls like a drum beat.

Suddenly Robyn stopped fighting and remembered the last time she'd been around that bird. Each clap cracked like a whip. Down in the other cell, the prisoner clanked his tankard against the bars.

In the cacophony of claps and clangs, the jackdaw hit the wall and tumbled down. Robyn darted out the cell and pulled the heavy door behind her.

"You'll hang for this!" Maudlin lunged for the cell door.

"Come on Joan!" Robyn made a dash for freedom.

The sound of heavy boots behind her meant Joan had to be close. At least, she hoped the sounds belonged to Joan. No time to turn and check. Another pair of boots joined them.

"The tower!" Joan panted as they came to a staircase.

Robyn heaved with relief that the folks behind her were allies not enemies.

Pain lanced her chest as they took the stairs two at a time. Tightness burned her thighs. Mouth-breathing all the way, Robyn kept running. When they reached the top, they gulped for air. Joan and Robyn leaned against the walls, their breathing loud and messy.

Gasping for breath, Georgia came into view.

"You two . . . are trouble."

"Sorry," Joan shrugged.

Robyn couldn't help smiling. "Can you get the tower door open?"

Georgia waved her hand in the air and wheezed, "Can't breathe."

They didn't have time for luxuries like breathing. By now,

Maudlin must've got her bird back, and her temper up. She only had to follow the direction of their noisy footsteps to know where they'd gone.

And set more guards on them.

"Georgia, how many guards does Maudlin have?"

Wheeze. Headshake. Joan splayed all four fingers and her crooked thumb out. "Only three."

Joan laughed, "Hey, my thumb's crooked like that too!"

Fresh tears made clean channels down Georgia's face. "I'm so sorry darling."

They hugged again.

They couldn't stand around here wasting time, they had to keep moving. Heartbeat still three times faster than normal, Robyn was as recovered as she'd ever be. "Give me the keys. I'll go to the tower."

With shaking hands, Georgia gave Robyn the keys from her belt.

Instead of charging straight off, Robyn stopped and made herself think. Made a plan. Once she found the tower, what then? She knew Maudlin would be furious at what they'd done, but she didn't have that many guards to do anything about it.

Which meant Robyn and her gang had the numbers.

As long as they didn't run into Roger of Doncaster. Then again, if she didn't get a move on, somebody would find them and they'd all end up in the dungeons.

Another flight of stairs, this lot took her down again, which felt like the wrong direction, but then she went up again, away from Joan and Georgia and far away from Maudlin. She stopped by a narrow gap in the wall where the wind howled through. Everything was made of timber up here. Creaking timber that groaned as the wind blew.

Timber that held within it centuries-old smells of life. The next door she came to had the unmistakable noises and aromas of people behind it. A great many people. And a cow? Yes, definitely the stench of cow behind the door. How had they even got it up here?

Creaking the door open, Robyn found herself staring at the rear end of Bella.

Her mother looked up from her stool by the cow and beamed. "Robyn darling!" Then her face fell. "They haven't sent you up here too, have they?"

Stunned, Robyn shook her head and looked around the room. "I'm here to get you out. All of you," she said. Only then did she notice how many 'all of yous' there were. The women and children from her village she knew straight away, but there were many more, including Joan's elderly parents and others she knew from Littleton. It wouldn't be fair to get her people out but leave the rest behind.

Eleanor left Bella mid-milking and locked Robyn in a hug. Mother Miller then appeared, flour over her face and hands, smothering her in a three-way hug. Four and five way, judging by the bodies clamouring around her.

She squeezed out, "No time for hugs, we have to leave."

"But we're nearly done." Mother Miller said.

The wind howled through the narrow windows. Several villagers worked together attaching a heavy quilt over it to block out the wind.

Candles burned in stone holders to shed light, but there were no fires like the Inn where they could keep warm. Surrounded by timber, a fire up here would incinerate them.

"We're making flour and butter to see Sheffield through the winter." Eleanor said.

"But we have to go. Now"

Mother Miller said, "We promised Maudlin we'd finish the work."

"Maudlin's a lying cow." Robyn said, then noticed the long-suffering beast and said, "Sorry Bella."

Mother Eleanor looked from the villagers to Robyn. "We made a deal that if we produced enough for the winter, we'd be able to stay. If we left now, what do we have to go back to?"

What did they have? Only the smithy still had a roof back in Loxley. Littleton fared even worse. Who knew what condition the other villages would be in. "She's keeping you here as prisoners!"

Mother Eleanor said, "As we have nowhere else to go, it's a moot point darling."

Robyn's head was going to explode in frustration. "I broke in here to get you out. And you want to stay?"

"If you've got any sense, you'll stay as well," Eleanor said. "Sheffield is our liege lord. We came here for help and we've received it."

Everyone was staring at her now and looking confused and guilty. Even the people not from her village–for there were dozens of women and children up here working. Sewing, milking, milling flour and churning butter. Where were Joan's parents? They had to be here somewhere. She splayed her hands out. "Doesn't anybody want to get out of here?"

The wall quilt rippled aside. Wind howled through the thin window, its icy teeth biting Robyn's neck. She pulled the hood over her head. Maybe her mother wasn't so crazy after all. At least staying here, they had a place to stay; warm blankets and plenty to eat. Much more than they had back in Loxley.

A knock came from the other side of the wall. From this height?

Mother Miller opened a hatch to reveal Marion sitting in a loop of rope, his face whiter than flour.

"We have a way to get you out," he said. "Then we can get Robyn out of the dungeon."

"I'm here," Robyn made a small wave.

"Oh, hi." A huge grin split his face, followed by red blooms on each cheek. "Well done you."

Robyn beamed with pride. Not just from Marion's compliment, but his hatred of heights. How he hadn't vomited yet was a miracle.

Joan and Georgia chose that moment to stagger in to the room. Joan sized up the room and said, "OK let's get everyone out in an orderly fashion before Maudlin calls in reinforcements."

Once more the wind howled through. It snuffed the candles, filling the air with waxy smoke.

"Joan? Is that you?" Her elderly parents approached.

Oy, the delays! Robyn wanted to slap them all upside the head.

Why where they not listening to her and doing exactly what she said?

Turning to Marion, she shrugged in futility as Joan's elderly mother hijacked the scene and loudly called out to her daughter. She took her sweet time reaching Joan, which only made Robyn agitate all the more to get out of there. Maudlin was coming!

But no, this would play out in parent-time, as Joan introduced her mother and father to Georgia. At which point, Marion climbed inside the window and Robyn helped him get his breath back. Credit where it was due, he'd done an incredibly brave thing.

"That took guts," she whispered as they closed the window slats.

He gave her a nudge. "How's the plan going?"

"It was going fine until just now." Robyn crossed her arms over her chest, then raised her voice to the room. "Can we get out of here? We can have reunions later."

"Robyn dearest," Mother Eleanor said, "All things considered, this is the best place for us to be."

"But Marion has gone to so much trouble!"

Breaking away from her father and both her mothers for a moment, Joan said, "Robyn's right. We should get out of here. Mum, Dad, Mum, come with me. Hey Marion, how does that sling work?"

Marion wedged the hatch open, cold wind raced through. His fingers clamped on the edge of the frame, his knuckles as white as his face. "Wilfred and Madge have the horses are down below, they're pulling on the rope, which goes up there through a couple of pulleys and holds you up and guides you down. Works great. Just don't look down, yeah?"

Joan reached the window and had a look out. "Oh dear. It is a long way. Are you sure it will hold me?"

It didn't seem possible, but Marion's face paled even more.

"Everyone out the window in an orderly fashion," Robyn said.

Joan stepped back from the window. "Shouldn't I go last, you know, just in case the rope, uh, you know?"

"Nobody else is going, Joan," Eleanor said.

Robyn gasped. "Mother! Stop ruining it. Maudlin will be here any second!"

"Well I'm not leaving," Eleanor said, sitting back down near Bella.

Something exploded inside Robyn. "You're choosing the cow? Over me?!"

"It's not like that," her mother said, making a little moue with her mouth. "But that is a long way down, and we're not prisoners. We're free to leave any time we like. There's no lock on the door."

The wind flapped the tapestries back and forth. Not many people made eye contact with Robyn. Those who did had looks of helplessness about them.

"But we went to so much trouble!" Robyn said. Hot tears welled in her eyes. No way would she leave without them. No way on earth would she . . . Dammit! The first drop splashed on her cheek, then the next. She swiped with her tunic sleeve and turned to Marion. "So much for plans then."

He looked equally crestfallen.

"Well Joan, you may as well climb out," Robyn said, every word dripping with defeat.

"That's a heck of a long way down. Can't we take the stairs?" Joan said.

"Come on," Marion guided Joan out the window, speaking softly with a reassurance that masked his own terror. *What a man!*

Joan looked back to her parents. "You're coming too, right?"

"Er," her father said, putting his arm protectively around his wife. "Might be best we stay here through the winter."

Joan's elderly mother turned to Georgia. "Our girl is so precious. Take good care of her."

Tears welling in her own eyes, Georgia nodded, then embraced them in a group hug. "Thank you so much. She's a lovely girl. Thank you."

Joan? Lovely? Robyn boggled as she watched her giant friend clinging to Marion as Wilfred eased the rope to lower them to the ground.

"I'm next out the hatch," Georgia said as she made her way to the window.

"Why don't you stay with us, Robyn dear?" Eleanor asked. "There are so many of us, Maudlin will hardly notice one more. We'll have plenty of bread and milk and be warm enough right through winter."

All this effort to find her village, and they didn't want to leave. How infuriating!

Marion appeared at the window hatch again. "Grannyma and Tuppence are safe at the sheep pens. Madge wants to stay with us." Then he handed over a small bag of gold coins. About half of the half Marion had split from the original bag.

"Thank you, Marion." Mother Miller's eyes grew round like plums. "My goodness, where did you ever get this?"

Marion scratched the back of his neck. "I wish there was more. Maudlin has the rest of it."

Mother Miller shoved the purse of coins under her apron. "Thank you," she said, giving Marion a heavy knitted shawl. "You'll need this more than me."

Next down the rope pulley was Georgia. They were going as fast as they could, but Maudlin could turn up at any moment.

From the safe ground below, Joan waved up to Robyn. There wasn't much room down there, what with the narrow path and the tall fence surrounding the tower keep. There was no room on the other side of the fence at all, just a long sloping hill all the way down. All things considered, Robyn was relieved she was breaking out, instead of trying to break in.

Robyn willed Marion to get back up to the hatch as fast as he could. Heavy footsteps sounded in the stairwell on the other side of the door. "Hurry Marion."

"You'll need this," Mother Eleanor said, holding the bow Robyn had fished out of the Littleton well. This time it was clean and freshly strung with a tight drawstring. And she had a quiver full of arrows.

Robyn threw her arms around her mother and wept into her neck.

Eleanor said, "Now you stay safe, you hear? And tuck in your frock before you climb out, don't want to get it caught on anything."

Robyn giggled. "You're the friar of tucks, and the tie-er of frocks."

"Be good Robyn," her mother smiled sadly. "And stay safe. And find somewhere warm. I will see you in Spring."

With another hug of farewell, Robyn slung the weapons over her shoulders and climbed out the hatch.

Only to become stuck because the bow was too wide to fit through the window.

"This is too perfect!" Maudlin said as she stormed in the room.

Panic overrode common sense. Robyn grabbed the weapons off her back and threw them out the hatch, hoping they'd land inside the fence below. As Maudlin stomped towards her, she climbed out, reaching for Marion.

The cold wind stole the grip from her fingers. She fumbled and slipped in Marion's arms. Couldn't find the loop in the rope for her foot.

"Hold on," Marion said as they swung in mid-air.

"Don't drop me!" Robyn cried out. She would have cried for real if the wind didn't rip her tears away before they came out.

"I've got you," Marion said.

The hatch rose in the air. Or, more logically, they dropped away from the wall. Maudlin leaned out the hatch, cursing them a good one.

Slipping down his body, Robyn wrapped her arms and legs as tightly around him as she could, locking her ankles and wrists around his middle.

"Nearly there."

An agonizing time later, they felt the soft thud of the ground underneath them.

"Marion, you were amazing!" Robyn smothered him in kisses.

He drew breath. "I'll try not to let my halo blind you."

"That must have killed you to be up that h–"

Marion shut her up with another kiss, then said, "We're safe on the ground, that's all that matters."

The ground. Frantically, Robyn looked around for the bow and arrows she'd tossed down. They were scattered about, muddy but not broken.

"Let's get going," Wilfred said, untying the rope from around Marion's torso.

"Well done on getting the horses and the wagon up here," Robyn said.

Marion shrugged the compliment aside. "Always good to have a plan."

Robyn placed her bow and arrow into the back of the wagon, where Joan and Georgia were sitting. Madge, Robyn noted, was sitting up the front in the seat next to Wilfred.

Icy winds brought with them the smell of wet soil and . . . smoke?

She and Marion looked at each other. "Do you smell that?" They said in unison.

Looking up, smoke puffed out the narrow tower windows and the hatch they'd climbed from.

It had to be some kind of terrible accident. Surely Maudlin wasn't so insane as to set fire to it?

Suddenly Mother Eleanor leaned out the hatch and called, "Robyn dear? Change of plans! Can we come with you please?"

CHAPTER 9

*W*arning horns and shouts filled the Sheffield air. As did billowing smoke. People ran from all directions, many of them with ladders. Some of them with buckets. Some of those buckets even had water in them.

"Marion, get off the rope, we'll be able to get two people down at a time if it goes up empty," Robyn said, holding the slack end and hoisting it upwards. Then she shouted up to the window, "Grab the rope! Climb on to the loop and grab someone to come down with you. All right?"

"Yes dear." Eleanor called back. "Do hurry!"

People with ladders arrived and leaned them against the walls. One person climbed up with a hatchet and cut wider holes where the narrow windows had been. People scrambled out the gaps and down the ladders. Before long, the tower was a sea of people climbing up and down, helping people to get out, tipping buckets of water in. It was a valiant effort, but Robyn feared the flames were too strong.

Marion and Wilfred's rope and pulley system managed two people down at a time, usually a trembling mother and wrapped-up-child.

"What about Bella?" Eleanor said as she patted herself down now that she was safely down.

Honestly, shouldn't people come before livestock? Timber creaked above them. In a harrowing "*whoosh*" the tower roof caught alight.

Fear curdled Robyn's stomach. "Please tell me everyone got out?"

Marion grabbed her in a hug. "It wasn't your fault."

Red mist covered Robyn's eyes. "I never thought it was!"

"Don't be so defensive!"

"I can't help being defensive when you're saying it's my fault!"

"I didn't say th–"

At which point screams for help rang out.

People were still trapped inside, desperate to get out. A human chain of people with water-filled buckets couldn't compete with the growing flames.

How had this even happened? Robyn fretted. Had someone knocked a candle over or had Maudlin deliberately lit it?

Desperate to help, Robyn and Marion joined in the human chain and hefted full buckets along the line.

A stampede of people and a mooing cow poured from the tower, bursting out into the fresh air. A cheer went up and news carried down the line that everyone was out.

Relief swept through Robyn, leaving her as soggy as wet bread.

"Let's get back to the horses and get out," Marion said.

No time to rest, Robyn scrambling up the hill to where Wilfred, Madge, Joan and Georgia stayed with the horses. Through the smoky haze, Wilfred's face shone like a red beacon of itchiness.

Robyn scratched her cheek in sympathy. "You all right."

Wilfred dragged his sleeve across his face. "Aa-djaw!"

"I'll take over if you like." Robyn relieved Wilfred of duty. Madge was beside him, her hands filled with sheep's wool to soothe his face and hands.

"I must be a mess," Will said.

Madge beamed. "You're my hero. Now let me look after you."

A half-hearted protest from Wilfred followed. Robyn was glad he had the wool over his eyes so he couldn't see everyone else making silly faces as Madge doted on him.

A stab of jealousy shot through. How come she and Marion couldn't be this nice to each other? They had the occasional lovely moment together, but then things turned tetchy and she wanted to kick him in the shins.

Thoughts of boy problems were quickly pushed aside as she took in the next hurdle facing them. Marion, Wilfred and Madge had done brilliantly to get themselves, the horses and the wagon up here in the narrow space between fence and the tower. But there was only one way down and it was packed with people running back and forth. Most were running away from tower, but a few brave or crazy people were running back in, desperate to salvage whatever they could from the burning building.

At least the stone part of the tower wouldn't burn, so the people of Sheffield wouldn't lose everything. Not like they had in Loxley.

"Everyone ready to leave?" Robyn looked back to her motley friends, all in various states of shock and exhaustion. They still had to get down from the hill, and it was quite an angle. "You'll have to get out of the wagon, the steps are too steep. Will and Marion, you two get the wagon down the steps. I'll guide the horses."

Plus One hardly needed guiding. She followed lock step with Marion and the others, but Shadow had very different ideas. The noise and movement of people rushing about, their arms full of flour bags, clothes, cheese wheels, butter and tools, spooked the horse. That was before Robyn even saw the steps they had to climb down.

"It's OK girl. I'm right here," she cooed, stroking the horse's nose. Reaching into her pocket, she found nothing of use to bribe her. An apple would be brilliant right about now. She scanned the base of the tower and found tufts of grass poking out. She ripped the grass, pulling it out roots and all. "Here you are darling. I'm going to guide you down the hill and you're going to be fine."

Straight down the steps wasn't going to cut it. The hill was incredibly steep, the steps narrow and clogged with people running up and down. "Easy girl. I won't let you go." Not that the horse would have any idea what she was saying, but Robyn hoped her soothing tone conveyed the message.

Shadow took a diagonal step. They were going down, the long way.

"Good girl. Now the next one."

Shadow walked across the face of the hill. Robyn walked beside Shadow all the way, her body on the lower side to protect the horse from slipping. And to keep guiding her downwards.

"Good girl!" Robyn said as they reached the fence on the other side. "Now turn around and we do it again."

Shadow dropped her head and nibbled grass growing near the step.

"Fair enough. I'm pretty hungry myself." She turned to see how the lads were getting on with the wagon and the other horse. They were half-lifting half-guiding the wheels over each step, careful not to jostle too hard.

A strange thing was happening. As people ran from the tower, they threw whatever they'd salvaged into the back of the wagon and then ran back in. *They think the wagon's part of the rescue.*

"Come on girl," Robyn clicked her tongue and guided Shadow diagonally down the face of the hill again, all the while giving her praise and compliments. They were half way down now, which wasn't a bad effort. They'd also caught up to the back of the wagon, so she could see what people were piling on to it. A bag of oats fell and spilled onto the ground. *Nice one.* Robyn scooped the oats into her palms and offered them to Shadow. The horse's whiskery lips tickled Robyn's palms, making her giggle. She turned to get more oats and found Marion and Wilfred had already moved on.

Lured by the oats, Shadow followed the wagon all the way down the hill to the flat ground of the bailey.

Brilliant!

"Right, are we all here?" Robyn said. "Everyone get on board."

There were so many of them. Wilfred, Marion, Madge, Mother Eleanor, Joan, Georgia and herself. They wouldn't all fit on the wagon.

A wagon now groaning with winter supplies. How could there be so much in reserve when the people of Sheffield looked so destitute?

With blinding clarity Robyn knew what she had to do.

Filled with a sense of purpose she scrambled to the top of the wagon and handed out supplies to people.

A window opened, revealing her future. A life that involved

looking after people and making sure everyone had what they needed. Why should people starve when others had too much?

With winter on the way, how could she do anything less?

The wind blew icy and cold. Robyn pulled her hood up to protect her ears as she handed food to the people. People who looked cold and thin and miserable. Their faces lit up as she passed a sack of–she had a quick look, it was kale–into a woman's grateful arms. An incredibly skinny woman with three children hanging on to her skirts.

"God bless you, child," she said.

Oh yes, this was absolutely the right thing to do. As if all her previous life experiences had led her to this very point.

A woman screamed with rage, breaking Robyn's wonderful fantasies of spending her life feeding the needy.

"What are you doing?" She raged.

Robyn knew that voice. It was Maudlin, even before she saw the black bird fly at a peasant to make her drop her sack of food. The peasant clung to the food as if it were a child to protect. Robyn grabbed a stretch of rope and whipped it in the air towards the crow. The end of the rope cracked with a deafening snap. The crow stopped attacking and wheeled around, then landed on the roof of the nearby buttery.

"Give that back! It's the property of Sheffield!" Maudlin stomped closer. The grim look on her face changed to outrage when she recognized Robyn. "You! I should have known you'd be at the centre of this!"

"Me?" Anger overflowed in Robyn. Instead of letting the anger rule her, she turned it against Maudlin. "You're the one who's crazy enough to set your own tower on fire!"

It was a gamble to accuse someone of deliberately starting a blaze. Silence snapped in the air around them. A palpable sense of "Did she really say that?" passed between everyone.

Robyn went even harder. "You're mental!" She kept grabbing bags of food and butter churners and wheels of cheese, passing them out to the crowd to share the goods.

Maudlin cried out, "You're nothing but a robbing hoodlum!"

"You're the thief!" Robyn yelled back. "Look at these people.

They're starving. They won't make it through the winter if they have no food. And the whole time you had my people up the tower working like . . . well, working like peasants."

"They *are* peasants!"

"You weren't going to share the food, were you? No matter how hard everyone here worked, there's no way you were going to look after them!" It's amazing how much poured from her mouth now that she was in a right temper.

At which point, Mother Eleanor handed Robyn the bag of golden coins. "I'm so proud of you darling."

The coins. Robyn felt all kinds of hypocrite as she looked at the coins. She was going to share them, but only with her people from Loxley. Maybe the people of Sheffield needed them more? Before she could change her mind, Robyn pulled the top of the bag open, then flung the coins out across the bailey. People scrambled over the ground to snatch them up.

The wagon below her jerked forward. Robyn lost her footing and buckled. Wilfred and Marion were hitching the horses into their harnesses. With another jolt they headed for the castle gates.

Finding her feet again, Robyn kept handing out food and other goods to whoever came near. It felt amazing to be giving people what they wanted. It also caused so much chaos immediately around the wagon there was no way Maudlin could get near them.

That horrid little crow landed back on Maudlin's shoulder. Despite the distance growing between them, the sight of that crazy woman and her jackdaw made things wobble in Robyn's tummy.

"Let's get out of here," she urged Marion.

Not that she was a coward. Not really. But the thought of taking on an angry Maudlin turned her knees to butter.

"Run away little girl. Run as far as you can," Maudlin yelled. "And when you get there, keep running!"

Ahead of them, the gates were still closed.

"Georgia, can you and Joan open them?"

Joan and her mother smiled to each other, then said, "Let's smash!"

THE SPLINTERED REMAINS of the Sheffield gates were long behind them. Robyn wasn't sure what road they were on, only that they were heading away from Maudlin.

"We're lucky Roger and his men weren't at the gate. We got off lightly." Marion said.

Oh sod! Robyn had forgotten all about him. The man who'd caused all their troubles in the first place. She called out to Wilfred and Madge, "Stop the wagon. We have to turn around."

"We are not going back to Sheffield!" Marion said.

"That's right. We're not," Robyn said. "We're going to Nottingham."

His eyebrows shot up. "But that's days away!"

Robyn nodded. "We have plenty of food to last us. I didn't give it all away. But we need to get to the Sheriff of Nottingham and tell him what's going on. Roger and his men are stealing in his name, trashing his reputation."

"We go all the way to Nottingham to tell the Sheriff what? That the people collecting his taxes are doing far too good a job of it?"

"Don't argue with me!" Robyn was getting monumentally fed up with the way Marion kept blocking her like this. Her ideas were like a path through the forest and his interruptions felled trees across it.

"I will argue with you because you're not making sensible plans."

"Plans don't work!" That red mist was back. "Plans only work when everyone goes along with it. And, hello, did you see what happened when I turned up to liberate everyone? They didn't go along with it!"

"Stop fighting, you two," Mother Eleanor butted in.

Both breathing hard, Marion dropped his voice low. "So now you're saying we front up to Nottingham with no plan at all and expect him, an Earl, to go along with what we say?"

"I don't know!" Robyn screamed at him.

"Then stop shouting at me because I'm only trying to help!"

Furious with herself and the world in general, Robyn made a guttural cry and flung her arms about. "Then everyone can stop looking to me for the answers because I don't have any."

Palms up in a 'will you calm down you're scaring the horses?' motion, Marion said, "We're looking to you because someone has to be in charge."

"Fine! From now on, Joan is in charge."

Shocked that she'd been drawn into the conversation, Joan said, "Why me?"

"Because . . . you're the tallest!" Robyn leapt off the wagon and stormed off into the shrubbery at the side of the road. There she flopped down in a bed of fallen leaves. Arms around her knees, she rocked softly back and forth. It made comforting scrunching noises beneath her. Not enough to drown out the sound of approaching feet.

Marion sat down beside her. "Everything is going to be all right," he said as he put his arm around her shoulder.

She shrugged him off. "How can it be? It's been one horrible thing after another."

The cool winds swirled the fallen leaves around their feet. Figuratively she loosened one of the constrictive bands around her heart. "I'm scared, Marion. I'm really scared."

He pulled her in for a warm hug. "If you weren't scared, you'd be doing it wrong. We're all here for you. We're all in this together."

The hug contained security and the promise of belonging. Another band slipped from her heart. "I used to dream of going on an adventure."

Marion nodded.

"But I don't want to any more. Adventures suck."

He hugged her again. "It only seems like that now. Because we're in the sucky phase and Roger and Maudlin want to hang us from a gibbet. But things will get better, I'm sure of it."

"Really?"

"Yeah." He got back to his feet and held his hand out to help her up.

"How can you be so sure?"

"Easy," he said as they stepped back to the road, "Things can hardly get any worse, can they?"

Back with her group, people rallied round with hugs and reassurances for Robyn. Mother Eleanor gave her the squishiest cuddle and said, "It will be all right, come on, let's get moving again."

Joan and Georgia declined a seat and walked a few paces behind, chatting away, catching up on lost time. Their long strides made it easy enough for them to keep up. Shadow, the showpony-turned-workhorse, kept right on marching with her horsey friend Plus One, pulling the wagon behind them.

Robyn felt sorry for the horses doing the heavy lifting. "I'm going to walk up the front," she said to nobody in particular.

"Tie your frock dear," Mother Eleanor said.

"Yes mother." She jumped over the side of the wagon, her tunic becoming caught in the wheel with a loud ripping noise.

"I told you to tie your frock," Eleanor said, quirking one side of her mouth.

Too tired to argue, Robyn tied the ripped edges of her clothes together and jogged over to Shadow. The horse wouldn't make comments or make her feel guilty. No. The horse was her friend and they understood each other.

On they walked, down the middle of the dirt road filled with small puddles from recent rain and general damp.

Behind her, Wilfred sneezed.

A scattering of "bless yous" rang out.

And again.

More "bless yous"–

Robyn counted five, four, three two–

And again.

Poor Wilfred. He'd been incredibly helpful, yet all he'd earned in return was a face full of rash. Madge doted on him, which was some compensation.

"We left Bella behind!" Eleanor cried out.

Robyn's shoulders slumped. "You can't be serious?"

"I am! She's more valuable than gold, that cow. What kind of a parent am I to forget my own child?"

With a silent 'how dare you', Robyn pursed her lips.

"You know what I mean!" Eleanor shifted sacks of food abot on the wagon. "Where's the rope? Please tell me we brought some rope? Come on don't just–oh!"

Mother leaped back in shock. Everyone stopped to see what cause the surprise. A sheepskin flapped to the side, revealing Ellen a'Dale underneath.

"Hiya," she said.

"What the devil are you doing here?" Robyn shouted.

"You've got a nerve," Eleanor said.

"I'm really sorry." Ellen put her palms up in surrender. "It was the only way I could think of to get away from Maudlin. She made me turn you in. I didn't have a choice, honestly. And I understand that you never want to see me again, so if you want to throw me over I'll be on my way."

"You what?" Marion stared daggers at her.

Yikes, Robyn was relieved Marion had never looked at her like that, the kind of look that said he wanted to whack her with a hammer.

"I won't lie to you, I did the wrong thing and I'm sorry," Ellen started. "I used your wagon to sneak out of Sheffield under Maudlin's nose, but I had to get away."

Marion's voice sounded low and deadly. "You've been working for Maudlin the whole time, you still are. You think we'll say, 'that's fine, off you go?' "

"I was hoping you'd forgive me and let me stay with you."

That brought guffaws of laughter from everyone. Even Wilfred looked like he was joining in. Or maybe his eyes were watering from being so close to the horse?

"I can't trust you as far as I can spit," Robyn said. "Get out of our wagon, you're on your own."

"Hang on a minute–" Marion interrupted.

"–Not plans ag–"

"–Raise your hands if you trust Ellen."

The cool wind blew through the bare trees either side of The King's Road. Leaves fluttered and formed drifts. Not a single person raised their hand. They could be waiting until the other side of winter and still nobody would raise their hand.

"It's not that I completely distrust you," Mother Eleanor said, trying to find some kind of compromise. "It's merely that you haven't given us a reason to put our trust in you. Do you see where I'm coming from?"

"I'll be on my way then. Nice knowing you." Ellen climbed out of the wagon and walked at a steady pace away from them.

"Should we go after her?" Eleanor asked.

Marion spoke Robyn's thoughts. "No thanks."

Robyn couldn't help thinking Ellen had left them far too easily. If the tables had been reversed, if she were the one being kicked out, she would have hung on to the wagon until they prized it out of her dead hands. Ellen hadn't even taken the sheepskin she'd been hiding under. *In this weather?* She had to be heading back to Maudlin.

As they urged Shadow onwards and they walked away, Robyn couldn't help thinking Ellen would betray them again. They turned the corner and Robyn eased Shadow to a stop. Drizzly rain began to swirl around them, adding a sparkly sheen to their tunics and hoods.

Marion looked at Robyn. "Do you think–?"

"–That was too easy? You bet." She said, "Joan, Georgia, turn the wagon sideways so the wind isn't blowing the horse hair into Will's face."

"Nice one," Wilfred said.

Pulling their hoods close around their faces to keep out the cold, Robyn and Marion walked quietly back down the road towards the last place they'd seen Ellen. The wind flurried around them, making it difficult to remain downwind the whole time. The thing about the wind, it not only carried smells, it carried (or blocked, depending on your direction) sound. Robyn's father had taught her this when they'd been hunting rabbits and ducks. Fish too. Apparently fish had an incredible sense of smell, so the only way to catch them was to cast lines upriver.

Being so close to winter, there were few leafy trees to hide behind. Only the random pine scattered deep in the forest. The leaves were crunchy and thick on the ground, so they couldn't step on those without making a racket.

Soon they saw hoof marks made by Shadow, and scuffs in the dirt where Ellen had landed and then walked off. The light was growing dim. They'd have to find her soon because if they wandered off into the Shire Wood, they'd become utterly lost.

And yet, they couldn't find Ellen.

"She can't have just vanished." Marion said, turning full circle, scanning hard for signs of her.

"I can't tell if these are fresh boot marks or not," Robyn said, looking at an impression on the ground. Not exactly an impression, more a removal of the top layer of dirt. The drizzle made everything sticky, so as they walked, their boots lifted a layer of road up with them.

They kept looking for signs, until finally: "That way," Robyn pointed into a space between trees where a muddy half-boot print *smushed* into the grass.

Marion dragged the side of his boot onto the road, to mark a line they'd be able to find on their way back. He made an arrow point on the end, in the direction of the rest of the wagon and their gang. "Let's go."

They took careful strides, Robyn scanning the ground and plants for signs of someone walking through. She kept sniffing the damp air on the off chance the girl's scent would carry. But her own snuffly nose wasn't up to the job. Shadow had a beautiful nose. She should have brought the horse.

In the end it wasn't her nose that lead them to Ellen, it was her ears. The lilting tune carried in the wind, growing louder as they closed in to find the traitor sitting in a clearing, preparing a meal of cured meats and oaten biscuits.

"Don't mind if we do," Marion stepped forward and reached for a slice of meat.

Ellen surprised them both by not looking the least bit surprised. "I knew you'd follow me. That's why I've made enough for three."

Shocked, Robyn missed her next step. "Pardon?"

"I had to sneak a ride with you, otherwise I'd have no way to get this stash back to Maudlin."

"Hang on a minute, this is ours," Marion started looking through the hoard. "Well, some of it's ours. I recognize these tankards."

"All tankards look the same," Ellen protested.

Marion held one of them aloft in the dying light and pointed out a hallmark on the underside. "These two 'ems' are mine. It means 'Marion Made'."

"Well then . . . you made them for Maudlin." Ellen made to snatch it back.

"And that's why they say, 'Welcome home father,' on them? I suppose she had them made for when her dear papa came home from the war?"

A hesitation, "I don't know. Yeah. Probably. Why not?"

"You're not even trying now." Robyn snorted. "Maudlin's father and grandfather are both long gone. How else did she inherit Sheffield Castle?"

Ellen's face fell, "How did you know that?"

It was hard for Robyn not to boast, it really was. "It's how things work."

"Shame on you both, taking advantage of a girl who can't read," Ellen said.

Pangs of guilt spiked Robyn's tummy. She was hardly better in the lettering department. "Why don't we drop the pretence and get everything out in the open."

Ellen made shapes in the ground with the toe of her boot. "To be honest, I'm not sure how to tell the truth these days."

A sigh from Robyn. "Start by telling us whose stuff this is?"

"It's Roger's. Well, not really Roger's but he and his gang took it from Littleton and Loxley and the other villages around these parts."

Marion asked, "Did you burn those villages too?"

Shush Marion, Robyn thought. They were on the verge of getting her to open up.

"I didn't set fire to anything. But to be honest I didn't stop them either."

"Thanks for nothing," Marion shot back.

Robyn said, "Marion, why don't you go through the goods and sort things out for us? You're ever so good at counting and sorting things."

A sigh from Ellen. "I couldn't stop them lighting the fires, not really, otherwise I would have stood out too much. It was bad enough being the smallest one in the gang. I pretended to be a boy so I could spy on Roger for Maudlin, because she doesn't trust him. She doesn't trust anyone. I don't know why, she's a good woman. Well, she was good to me. Maudlin took me in when I had nowhere else to go. Life with her was lush. So when she asked me to do her a favour, I won't lie to you, it felt good to be needed. To have something to do. So I joined Roger when she asked me."

"So, you're working for Maudlin, and you're working for Roger?"

"Yes, but Roger doesn't know."

"He doesn't know you're working for him?"

"No silly, he doesn't know I'm working for Maudlin. He thinks I'm a boy. He thinks you're a boy as well. I knew it was girls who whacked us on the King's Road that night. If it makes you feel any better, he told Maudlin we were set upon by a huge gang of outlaws."

Roger knew her real identity after the way he looked at her in the dungeons. "In any case, he knows I'm a girl now."

"Does he now? Well, he lied and said there were ten of you or more at the time. He only said that to Maudlin to cover up for how pathetic he was at getting a belting from two girls. Then next time we were out–" she held her fingers up to make quote marks in the air, "collecting taxes" then she put her fingers down, "–He packed some of it away and hid it here, to come and get next time."

Robyn creased her brows, "What are those finger things?"

"I don't know, to be honest. Must have picked up the habit from Maudlin."

The girl was utterly baffling.

"At some point," she prattled on. "Roger will come back here and take this and keep it for himself. But of course, it belongs to Maudlin, so we can take it back to her in the wagon and then she'll be happy, and she'll forgive you for taking the food and you'll see how nice she can be."

"But this is our stuff!" Marion held up a packed crate of metallic goods that clunked and clanked as he carried them. "No way are we giving this to Maudlin."

Panic filled Ellen's face. "Oh! But we have to give it to her. That's the only way I'll get back in her good graces."

"You're serious? She's a raving banshee."

"I know, Robyn. But she's my raving banshee and I loves her."

Robyn and Marion shook their heads again. They packed what they could and carried it back to the road. As they reached the edge of the Shire Wood, they had yet another hurdle to overcome.

Roger of Doncaster stood there, hands curled into fists. And he looked none too happy about someone trying to steal his previously thieved items.

CHAPTER 10

*a*ny moment now, Roger would order his men to arrest them. Darkness settled about them; a blessing and a curse. He'd have to get closer if he wanted to lay a hand on Robyn, and she and Marion were fast enough to make a run for it. But they didn't know this part of the Shire Wood very well. They might make a run for safety, but they could just as easily charge off and brain themselves on a tree.

"We'll take those now." Roger reached his hand out to Marion.

"They're mine." He said.

Roger looked peeved. "I think you'll find they're mine."

Ellen interrupted. "I think you'll find they're Maudlin's, to be honest."

"Whose side are you on?" Robyn and Marion said together.

"Who in God's name are you?" Roger asked as he looked at Ellen.

"You don't recognize me?" Ellen asked.

"Should I?" He shot back.

"I worked for you for long enough. I took a belting for you. You left me here to look after your commission."

Roger stood there on the rise, squinting at her. "Allan?"

"It's Ellen really. I won't lie to you, I was only pretending to be Allan."

Roger shook his head in frustration. "You've dobbed me in good and proper to the witch, have you? Fine then, we'll still be taking this but we won't bother returning to Sheffield."

Silently, a large shape appeared behind Roger as he talked. Robyn wanted to look, but dared not in case she gave something away.

"Come on lads, there's work to—"

The large shape belted something hard into the side of Roger's head, sending him sprawling into the fallen leaves below. His men shouted in alarm and tried to spring into action, but they too were set upon from all sides.

Thwacks and whacks filled the forest, followed by grunts and moans. Everything happened quickly yet Robyn took in the detail. The newly reunited Joan and Georgia worked like they'd trained together all their lives, their fighting styles felling Roger's men with strokes strong and sure. One started to put up a fight with Joan but Georgia clonked him from the side.

The giants 'high-fived' each other for a job well done.

The fighting over, Robyn dashed over to make sure Roger was still alive. She put her ear to his mouth and felt his soft breath tickle her skin. Yes, alive, but completely unresponsive.

"Nicely done." Marion gave Joan a fist-bump.

"Little help?" Robyn called out, holding Roger by the feet and needing someone to carry the other end of him.

Georgia stepped over to her. "Leave it with me, love," she said, putting down her tree branch weapon and hauling the floppy Roger over her shoulder in one scooping motion.

They loaded the knocked-about men into the back of their cut-off wagon. Wilfred sneezed so loudly it shook the last leaves from the trees.

What did they do with all these injured attackers? They couldn't leave them here, they'd freeze. The only option was to take them back to Sheffield.

That's when Madge struck a flint and lit a candle inside a dirty lantern. A lantern hanging inside a plush carriage with the Earl of Derby's colours on the doors.

"I've got a plan," Madge said with a beaming smile. "Let's load the good stuff in this carriage, and hook Shadow and Plus-One up to it. Then we can haul Roger and his men in the wagon behind us?"

"I like it," Robyn said. "We'll head back towards Sheffield and leave these rotters by the gate. Then we'll make our way in the other carriage to Nottingham and give it back to the Sheriff."

"Can we give the horses back too?" Wilfred said, then sneezed.

That meant saying goodbye to Shadow. Unless Robyn could stay with the horse? After all, the Sheriff was also an earl, and earls probably had stables as big as the entire village of Loxley. Maybe one more peasant working in the stables wouldn't be noticed?

Ellen held a tree branch aloft. "Whose stick is this long-staff?"

"Mine," Georgia said, taking it back and placing it across the driver's seat of the carriage.

"I can drive the carriage if you want," Wilfred said.

Madge put her hand to his arm. "No Will, you're in here with me." She dragged Wilfred inside with a giggle.

Robyn rolled her eyes and climbed up to the driver's seat. Hang on. "Where's Ellen?"

"I'm on this one," she called out, indicating she was travelling with Joan and Georgia and Roger's men.

"No Ellen, you're with us," Mother Eleanor said, dragging her off.

From below her seat, Robyn heard Madge groan her disappointment that she and Wilfred wouldn't be left alone after all.

Ellen moaned, "But why can't I go back to Sheffield?"

"Because," Robyn said from her perch, "You'll tell Maudlin we're going to Nottingham, won't you?"

"Oh no, I wouldn't say that."

"Yes you would."

Ellen's shoulders slumped. "Well, yes, I probably would. But I'd give you a day's head start at least."

"Sorry, can't let you do it. You're staying with us whether you like it or not," Robyn said. "All right, is everyone on board?"

"Yes." They answered.

Shadow didn't want to move on without Robyn. "It's OK, Shadow, I'm right behind you." Robyn climbed down from the driver's seat and made her way to the front. "Easy girl," Robyn rubbed the horse's nose and gave her a kiss. "I've been on my feet all day too and I'm ready for a nap. Once we take these varmints back to Sheffield, we'll have a good rest, OK?"

Shadow seemed none too impressed as Robyn gently held her bridle and guided her in the right direction. "We'll not go all the way to Nottingham tonight."

She wasn't sure if she were speaking for the horse's benefit or her own.

"Er, Robyn?" Marion called out.

"What?" It was enough she had to put one foot in front of the other, much less answer Marion's irritating questions.

"We should take the South Road."

"We're on it, aren't we?"

Noisy creaks sounded behind her as Marion left his post and caught up. Soon enough, he fell in step beside her. "No, we were on the road going west from Sheffield, then we turned around, which means we're now going east. Towards Sheffield."

"Where is this South Road then, and how to we get on it?"

"We went past it as we left Sheffield. I don't think we've come back to it yet, but we need to keep an eye out for it."

"How are we going to see it? I can barely see my feet in front of me."

"I was thinking. Horses always know their way home. Shadow belongs to the Earl of Derby, and he's in Nottingham, so Shadow will know how to get to Nottingham."

"Really?"

Marion dropped his voice even lower. "Maybe not. But I'll keep an eye out for milestones because eventually we'll find one that points to Nottingham."

Milestones. Signposts. Another reminder that she couldn't read. But also, Robyn found herself feeling grateful that he hadn't been shouting the conversation from his seat on the carriage.

Oh, the carriage.

"Marion, who's driving?"

"Nobody, but you're leading Shadow anyway, so it hardly matters."

"In which case, can you lead Shadow for a bit? I'm stuffed."

Marion chuckled under his breath and let her go. Robyn timed it so she could climb up onto the front of the carriage while it was still moving. Her feet burned with relief as she lay horizontal across the driver's seat. Every muscle cried in protest but she fell asleep almost before she'd closed her eyes.

ROBYN WOKE but couldn't move. Every limb felt like wood as it slowly creaked to life. Rubbing the crust from her eyes, she looked out to see they were in a glade in the middle of the forest. The sun made fingers of light through the bare trees. Her head felt cold and her neck had seven kinds of kinks in it, but she was rested, and for that she was grateful.

"Morning," Marion said with a wink as he tented more branches over a fire.

"Morning." With creaking bones and tight muscles, Robyn climbed down from the driver's seat. "Where are we?"

"Not exactly sure. We left Roger and his men near the Sheffield Gates, then we took the South Road. Soon after that, Shadow cracked it with me and wouldn't go any further."

"How far are we from Sheffield?"

"Four milestones. The road's over that way," he pointed his thumb over his shoulder. "This seemed as good a place as any to rest."

A few stretches and yawns later, Robyn sat by the fire that Marion had made. He presented her with a tin plate piled high with fish for breakfast.

"This is amazing?" Manners be hanged, Robyn ate and talked at the same time. "How did these end up in the bags?"

"They didn't. I caught them from the stream this morning," he said with a prideful grin.

"Catch some more, they're delicious!" Robyn held her plate out for Marion to refill.

"Already on it. I've got Joan and Georgia building us a shelter further in the woods, and your mother and Ellen are catching more fish as we speak."

"What about Will and Madge?"

"They're busy." Marion turned bright red, showing Robyn exactly how busy those two must be.

"Right. So," Robyn accepted the refill of food and shoved it in her mouth. It was so perfect and buttery and melty. She pulled a bone out.

"Sorry, thought I got them all out."

"I like the bones, they're good," Robyn said, using it as a toothpick. "Heavens! I feel so much better. I'm sorry I've been snapping at you so much."

"We've all been beyond hungry."

"Yeah. That must be it." Robyn shucked the last remnants from between her teeth. "Any more?"

"There will be when your mother and Ellen get back."

The mention of the girl's name was such a downer. "What are we going to do with her?"

"We can't let her go, because she'll run straight back to Maudlin and tell her what we're up to."

"Why can't she be nice, like us?"

Marion laughed out loud.

"Don't mock me!" Robyn threw her empty plate at Marion, who caught it.

"I'm not making fun, I'm sorry. But Ellen probably thinks Maudlin is the nice one. She probably thinks she's doing the right thing by sticking with her. Maybe she thinks we're the bad ones here."

"How can making sure other people don't starve through winter be the wrong thing?" Robyn rose and wiped her hands on her tunic. Stretching again, she looked around their new surroundings. In this forest clearing, Shadow and her horsey friend Plus One chomped at the grassy tufts growing by the river. The water flowed bright and clear.

She took a few steps towards the damp shore and swished her hands in the icy stream. It was so cold her fingers could have cracked off, but she filled her palms and took a good slurp. Ice filled her chest and her head ached, but she slurped some more anyway.

"So, I was thinking," Marion said, coming up beside her and taking a few sips of his own. "This is a good spot. Plenty of fish, loads of fresh water. We've got supplies to keep us going for a while . . ."

"You didn't think of that just then, did you?"

His face fell. "How could you tell?"

"Because I can see Joan and Georgia from here." She waved at the women upstream who were building something against a tree. Something amazing and solid and potentially big enough to last them all through the winter. They had to have been working at that since sunrise.

Marion offered a compromise. "We could head straight to Nottingham if you want?"

Robyn sat on her heels. "You're being far too nice. And I've been a right cow."

Marion held back a smile.

Robyn slapped him playfully on the shoulder. "You were supposed to say I haven't been that bad."

This time Marion laughed outright.

A STICK of cold charcoal from the fire made an excellent crayon. Robyn drew a small circle on the trunk of a tree and coloured it in, then she drew a larger circle around it, and another, until the curve of the trunk made it difficult to create any more circles with any kind of accuracy.

"Looks dead easy," Marion said.

"It's supposed to be." Robyn replied. "That's why it's called practice. We'll get some shots in, then taking steps further and further back until we can't hit it any more. Then we'll move on to this." She pointed upwards. Marion followed her pointed finger and saw a bag filled with mud and twigs, hanging from rope.

This bag also had a charcoal target drawn on it, but the folds in the bag wobbled the lines.

"I'll tell you now, I don't have a hope of landing an arrow on that." Marion said.

Robyn couldn't hold back a smirk. "You have so many other things on your 'To do' list?"

"Point taken," Marion said, taking a look around.

They were in the Shire Wood, Sheffield was long behind them. They had food and temporary shelter, full bellies and nobody chasing them down this very minute.

"OK. We start with the easy target on the tree?" He asked.

"You can stand as close as you like, get your eye in, then we can start moving further back."

For the next long while—neither kept time, but it felt like a good session—they took turns at the bow and arrow, aiming for the tree, either hitting the target or hitting very close to it. Most of the time they hit the tree, which saved them searching the forest for lost arrows.

Later, the tree oozing sap from its wounds, they moved on to the mud bag. Arrow after arrow whizzed through the air. Some made a passing glance, most missed.

Robyn pierced the bag once, the arrow ripping a hole in it before falling to the ground.

"You are amazing at this," Marion said as they searched for lost arrows along the forest floor. "When did you learn to shoot?"

"Father taught me." Her shoulders slumped with a heavy sigh. "A couple of springs ago. We caught rabbits in the Shire Wood and brought home the biggest we'd had in years."

"I remember that! There was so much food, the only place big enough to cook everything was the forge! My father grizzled about the smell in the smithy."

Robyn laughed at the memory. "He didn't complain about the food though."

"Too right." Marion licked his lips and his eyes drifted towards the trees as he recalled the memory. "Do you think we could catch some now?"

The relaxed banter between them felt right. Friends being friendly. Marion wasn't making her feel remotely guilty about how badly things had turned out in Sheffield. In fact, he'd been a total gentleman and hadn't mentioned it.

"Sure. How's your shoulder feeling from the workout?"

He rolled a shrug to get his arm moving again. "Nothing a bit of roast rabbit can't fix."

"Let's get one then."

They collected oats to use for bait, then found a clearing near the stream and made sure they stayed down wind so they wouldn't be sniffed out. They also stayed as quiet as possible so they wouldn't be heard. Clever things rabbits, they could hear for miles on account of those massive ears.

After an age of waiting, the only animals that took the bait were pigeons. Bored and sore from crouching, Robyn loosed an arrow and pinned one bird with a perfect kill-shot.

"Better than nothing I guess," she said with a shrug.

They cleaned and plucked the bird by the stream.

Marion sighed heavily. "I miss Father. And although they annoyed the tripe out of me, I'm starting to miss my brothers as well."

"Me too. I wish the stupid Crusade was over. Then we'd go home."

Marion rubbed his shoulder. It had been a long afternoon of target practise. Then again, he was used to wielding a hammer on the forge, so he shouldn't be that sore.

Maybe he pretended to be injured? To save her feelings.

That time she'd seen him without sleeves at the forge, seen the definition in his arms. Yep, definitely fit. He had to be pretending for her sake.

"One pigeon won't go far among eight of us. We should catch more to share." He said at last.

"And waste more oats? We need to ration what we've got. We'll try this one first and see if it's any good before we hunt any more."

"Save our resources. Good idea," Marion said as they walked back.

As their camp came into view—the carriage to one side, a half-built shelter on the other, Robyn pulled up short. Regret clogged her throat. "We're outlaws now, aren't we?"

Marion scratched the back of his neck and then nodded. "Could be worse. At least we're not homeless."

Ahead of them, they heard singing. It was Ellen and Eleanor, making up songs as they sat around the campfire. Her mother sang:

ROBYN IN A HOOD
Does a lot of good
Robs from the rich and gives to the poor
Lives in the Shire Wood

"I LOVE IT MOTHER ELEANOR," Ellen said, "you truly have a gift for lyrics."

"Thank you," Eleanor said.

Robyn ground her teeth at how obviously Ellen was trying to get into her mother's good graces.

"She'll not replace you, if that's what you're worried about," Marion said.

Robyn glared at him. How dare he read her thoughts!

"Steady on," Marion held his palms up in surrender. "It's a good thing your eyes aren't arrows, otherwise I'd be deader than the pigeon."

The small bird didn't take long to cook, and neither did the fish.

"Tastes like greasy chicken," Joan said as she nibbled the pigeon drumstick.

Divided between eight of them, the bird offered no more than a bite each.

It was a tough and gamey bird, just like the season. In spring, fresh growth ensured rabbits and birds were fat and delicious. But now they were using up their fat reserves in the cold weather, and their muscles had turned to string.

"There are still so many fish," Ellen said. "I stood downstream where the water tumbles over rocks. As the fish swam near me, I flicked my hands under their bellies and tossed them onto the shore. Mother Eleanor sat on the shore and bagged them quick smart."

Everyone except Robyn and Marion murmured their congratulations as they chewed the scant meat off the pigeon bones.

"It's given me an idea," Ellen said. "Why don't we build a holding pen, here in the river? I can toss fish in there and we can feed them with oats, and then next time we need supper, we need only grab the fish we already have in the pen?"

It sounded like an excellent idea to Robyn, which made her instantly suspicious because the idea was Ellen's. The girl had to be up to something.

"I like it," Madge said. "Especially as the river's only going to get colder as winter moves in."

Ellen looked excited to have one person on board. "The river could freeze entirely. It's only a stream to be honest. Bagging the fish now will stop us starving later."

"But what if the fish freeze in the pen?" Robyn asked.

"Then they'll take a little longer to cook," Ellen said.

Mother Eleanor brightened. "Does that mean I won't have to sit near the water anymore?"

Right now, they had plenty of fish to share, so none of them would starve. But in a few weeks, would they still have food? As sure as night followed day, winter followed autumn. What would they do then?

As much as she hated to admit it, Marion was right. They needed a plan to survive the cold months ahead. Otherwise they'd all freeze and starve.

"Does anyone want that last bit of pigeon?" Joan asked.

"Help yourself," Robyn handed over her half-eaten pigeon thigh. "How about you Georgia?"

"I'm fine thanks," she said, picking her teeth with a wing bone. "I prefer the fish. I like Ellen's idea. Could save us all a lot of heartache later."

"Stomach ache, more like," Wilfred said as he handed his uneaten pigeon to Joan.

"Fish is better for your skin at any rate," Madge said, linking her arm with his.

How strange that Robyn felt she could trust an outsider like Wilfred, but not Ellen. Then again, Wilfred hadn't betrayed them.

As the sun dipped behind the trees, Mother Eleanor added more logs to the fire to build it up.

Ellen started singing again.

ROBYN IN A HOOD . . .

HEAT ROARED up Robyn's neck. She pulled the edges of her hood over her face. "Sing about someone else."

"Come on Robyn, it's a great song. You'll be famous," Ellen said.

"It is catchy," Mother Eleanor said.

Robyn said, "I don't want to be famous."

"Fine then. Let's sing about . . ." Ellen looked around the group, "Little Joan!"

"I'm not little!" The giant protested.

LITTLE JOAN with a staff of gold
Would not do as she was told

"I DON'T HAVE a staff of gold!" Joan threw her hands up.

"Poetic license," Ellen said as she kept going.

MET WILL SCARLETT on the road
Yes she met him on the road
And what did they do upon the road?
The battled each other with staffs of gold.

"NOW YOU'RE JUST MAKING NOISE!" Joan said.

"Am I really that red?" Will asked Madge. Madge shook her

head and cuddled him a little more. Then they said something quietly to each other and walked off to the carriage.

ROBYN and the merry friends
Travelled the wood from end to end
Robbed from the rich and gave to the poor
That's what the Robbing Hoods are for
We can't forget there's Georgia Green
Along with Joan the two are seen
The favourites in the group by far
Travel with Robyn wherever they are
Among the friends was the tie-er of frocks
Soon to be known as Friar of Tucks

"THAT DOESN'T EVEN MAKE SENSE!" Robyn put her hands over her ears. Ellen had a sweet voice and all, but the song was getting silly.

Timber creaked noisily beside her. The carriage was . . . rocking.

"Marion, you see that?"

Marion's eyes widened to show he had. "Will and Madge?"

Heat spread through Robyn.

Then they heard Madge's high-pitched voice. "Oh, stupid thing! Get in!"

"Nearly there." That was Wilfred.

Then some grunting. Robyn didn't know where to look. The ground suddenly held enormous interest as she stared at a small rock.

She must be redder than Wilfred after being near the horses.

"We can hear you out here," Marion said.

"Good," they heard Madge grunt. "Get in here and help us out."

Marion and Robyn boggled at each other, knowing their minds were both way down in the mud. "Er, help?" Robyn asked, her voice cracking in the middle.

Another grunt from the carriage.

"Are you both all right?" Marion called out. He didn't take a step any closer to the carriage though.

Mother Eleanor spoke up. "Go on then, they obviously need you."

At which point, Wilfred shambled out of the carriage and waved them over. "It's this last bit, then we're done."

Confused and apprehensive, Robyn and Marion walked towards the carriage.

Way back when her father used to be around, she'd heard her parents making strange noises and knew exactly what it was. She'd grown up around plenty of animals and witnessed season after season of babbies and calves and goats in the village.

"Oh!" Marion cried out as he looked inside, then staggered backwards, laughing.

"What?" Robyn stepped closer.

Inside the carriage, Madge had bundled branches across the width of the foot well, to build it to the height of the seats to form a large bed for several people. They were trying to get the last couple of timber wedges in to hold it all in place, but they'd shoved the sticks in so badly it would end up being incredibly uncomfortable. They wanted to take everything apart and start again, but now they'd dislodged some of it, the rest of the branches wouldn't come loose.

"Oh!" Robyn said, as she finally made sense of the situation.

Marion grabbed at the sticks and pulled with all his might. The carriage rocked violently.

That would explain all the rocking and swaying then. And the grunting. Forcing the branches out was the reason for the grunting.

"Whey!" They all cheered as the jammed branch came loose. Everything else could come out and they could start again.

Drizzle swirled, coating everything with shiny dampness as they worked to get the large bed right the second time around. Instead of rounded branches, Marion fetched an axe head and sliced some of them straight down the middle to create a flat edge.

Drizzle turned into showers as they worked on. Steam swirled with each breath. Showers deepened into steady rain. Making a comfortable shelter became a priority.

Back in the village, the smithy would have offered warmth and a place to dry out. But here in the woods, until Joan and Georgia could finish the round house, the carriage offered the only sure roof over their heads.

Shadow and Plus One shook the rain from their hides and carried on eating grass. It wasn't raining so hard, just the usual early winter cloak of misery. But if the rain grew heavier, surely the horses would feel it?

In which case, the animals needed a proper shelter as well.

"What's wrong?" Marion asked as he sliced another branch through the middle.

"We can't keep the horses." How her heart bruised to say that. Two less horses would be two less mouths to feed. Sure they ate grass, but they needed oats as well. Oats from a bag already quarter gone.

"They're not tethered," Marion said as he split another branch and handed the halves to Wilf. "They're free to go home any time they like.

Wilfred and Madge were creating an impressive cot. It would fit six people in a squeeze, but they had eight.

"I'm going to see how Joan and Georgia are getting on."

On the way she passed Mother Eleanor, dragging another branch over the fire. The branch was wet from sitting on the Shire Wood floor. It spat and bubbled as it burned. Thick smoke rose. Coals hissed with every sploshed raindrop.

"Tie your frock, it's dragging on the ground." Eleanor said.

"Tie your frock," Robyn mimicked as she trudged past.

In the stream, she found Ellen shaking and shivering as she secured her wicker trap. The poor girl's lips purpled from cold.

"You've done plenty for now. Go and thaw out by the fire," Robyn said.

"But I'm nearly done."

"You're nearly dead. Go warm up."

Ellen wedged another rock against her half-completed fish farm and sloshed out of the river. Her teeth chattered as her soaked body came into contact with the wind.

Concern pinged Robyn. The girl couldn't be trusted, but she was also doing her best. If they let her go they'd have one less mouth to feed and one less person to keep warm and dry. On the other hand, if they let her go, would she turn them all in to Maudlin?

Did they give her another chance? Maybe that was the right thing to do.

"Joan? Georgia?" Robyn called out as she approached the two giants working together.

"Hey Robyn, look what we've done." Georgia said, taking a step back to show their work.

They'd done something amazing, that's for sure. They'd rammed guide branches into the soft wet ground and woven thinner, green branches between them, creating an impressive round house with a small opening for the door. Above it, they'd made the framework for a roof. A roof that didn't have a hope of keeping the rain off in its present state.

Staying in it tonight would be impossible.

But soon.

"Brilliant." She kept her teeth closed to stop them from chattering. Her soaked hood dripped water down the back of her neck, each drip chilling her that little bit more until she felt like she could scream.

Why couldn't this adventure have happened in summer? Not that the rain always held off anyway, but at least in summer the branches were full of leaves that offered more shelter.

Why hadn't they stayed in Sheffield? Working in the tower for no reward might have been preferable to this misery.

"Cheer up love," Georgia said as she shook the droplets from her hood. "It's only rain."

Shadow and Plus One ambled over to see what they were up to. Robyn couldn't help giving her horse a gentle rub on her wet nose. Both horses shook themselves, sending water droplets in all directions. Their manes and tails were soaked through.

"Oh dear," Joan said as she looked at the two large animals. Large, soaked animals. "Get them in, it's a little drier at least."

"Come on," Robyn said, "Let's go warm up by the fire."

As they stood around the flames, Robyn suggested their sleeping arrangements. "Will and Madge have converted the carriage. We'll sleep in that until the roof on the round house is watertight."

But there was no way they'd all fit in the carriage. Not eight people, two of them giants at that.

Marion said, "We can sleep underneath." The 'we' included Robyn because he made an off-hand gesture and a shrug, as if it meant nothing.

Robyn kept her eyes down so nobody else would see how much the statement affected her. She missed what Marion said next but it ended with, "The carriage has been in the same place for so long, it's dry on the ground below." As dry as it could be this time of year.

"I'll sleep on the ground," Ellen said.

"Nice try," Robyn said out loud before she could reel the words back in.

"Nice try at what?" The girl looked affronted.

"Come on, Ellen, as soon as the rest of us are asleep you'll scarper back to Maudlin."

Hands on hips, Ellen protested her innocence. "In the dark? In the rain?"

"You'd probably take a horse while you were at it." Robyn said.

"Don't give her ideas," Marion kept his voice low.

But maybe a small part of her wanted Ellen to leave, and take the other horse with her. Not Shadow, obviously. Shadow was hers now. All the same, Ellen was crazy if she thought they wouldn't keep watch over her. "You're sleeping in the carriage" Robyn said, "We'll take turns staying awake and keeping an eye on you, so you can't get up to anything."

"I've frozen myself to the bone to get you fish for supper and you don't trust me." Fat tears rolled down her face like slugs.

"You've got a long way to go before you earn our trust," Marion said. Warmth spread through Robyn knowing she had Marion's full support.

"Darling, I think we should be the ones to sleep on the ground," Mother Eleanor said, casting a look between Robyn and Marion. "We need Marion in the carriage to keep an eye on Ellen."

Everyone except Mother Eleanor climbed into the carriage. Robyn opened the door to bid everyone goodnight. And to check they were all in there. It was a hot mess of warm, smelly bodies and damp clothes. Jealousy spiked her.

"Where's Ellen?"

"Under here," the girl said. She'd wedged herself into the foot well underneath them. Smart move. She'd be toasty warm in the crawlspace. It left plenty of room for five others to lie above her.

"Let's get some rest," Mother Eleanor said.

Bone weary, Robyn and her mother crawled under the carriage and clung to each other to keep warm.

"I wish the cow was here," Robyn said.

"Me too," Mother Eleanor said on a sigh.

"She's lovely and warm, isn't she?"

Mother Eleanor shifted again and squished herself into Robyn. "You're not . . . jealous of a cow, are you?"

"Course not," she said too quickly.

"I love you so much my darling," Mother said as they tried to get comfortable and failed. "I have said too much about Bella lately. I don't know why. Maybe I'm having a hard time adjusting to all the changes going on, what with your father being away. Lord knows what Crusades are for anyway. I don't even know how you can go to war against a belief system. I'll tell you now, no good can come of it."

It must be exhaustion making her eyes go funny, because a tear splashed out onto Robyn's cheek. "I miss father so much. Why aren't they back yet?"

"I wish I knew."

"How long do Crusades take anyway?"

"I haven't a clue. Try not to think about it, OK?"

Robyn grumbled and wriggled and tried—and failed—to get comfortable.

Mother Eleanor kissed the back of her head. "You must know I'm so proud of you for all that you're doing."

"Really?"

"Yes, really."

After that, the night didn't feel quite so cold and miserable.

CHAPTER 11

o surprise. In the morning, it was still raining. Robyn lay curled with her mother, watching puddles under the carriage ripple with each splash. Her back was vaguely warm from their shared body heat, but she couldn't feel her feet and her shoulder ached to the marrow from sleeping on her side all night.

It had all felt so simple and wonderful during their escape from Sheffield. She'd been handing out sacks of food to starving people, and it felt good. Like the time after she and Joan battled Roger's men on the road, then returned their goods to Loxley. She'd felt like a hero.

Now she felt cold, miserable and sore all over as the reality of 'being a hero' sank in. Wood creaked above them. The carriage rocked and swayed. The horses walked out from the round house and shook water from their coats. This is my life now, Robyn thought, as a warm tear left a cold trail down her face as it met the morning air.

Another tear followed the first, then the other eye let loose and there was no point stopping them. Nobody could see her, and she wasn't crying, just weeping to herself. Weeping for the lost security of Loxley, weeping for the unknown life that lay ahead. Weeping for the warmth of her bed.

"It's all right love," Eleanor said as she woke up. "At least we're all togeth–ow!" She clonked her head as she sat up.

Robyn wiped her face with the side of her hood. The creaking of the carriage above them matched the creaking in her joints as she snake-crawled her way out from underneath.

The carriage door opened. A tired and inelegant Joan tumbled out. "All right?"

"I'll get there," Robyn said, rolling her shoulders and yawning. This was every kind of miserable. "How did you sleep?"

"Couldn't have been as bad as you." Joan said with a shrug and a yawn chaser. "At least there's no frost."

"Rained too much for that," Robyn said.

"Good morning," Ellen said in her singsong way as she pulled herself out of her sleeping hutch. "That was lush. Never been so warm."

How dare she be so happy!

"Still raining then? Reminds me of home," Ellen pulled her hood over her head and had a stretch. "Right then, let's see if I can't get the fish farm up and running then."

"The fire must have gone out. I'll get the flint," Marion said as he climbed over Georgia to get out.

The fire. Their only source of warmth. Now the ashes were sitting in a puddle of rainwater. Misery sat like a heavy stone in the pit of Robyn's stomach as she watched Madge, Wilfred and Georgia climb out of the carriage, their expectant faces turned to Robyn in an unspoken chorus of, "What's next?"

Robyn's gave no cheer. "I have absolutely no idea."

"We need exercise," Joan said, giving Robyn a hard pat on the shoulder. "Come with me."

The last thing on Robyn's to-do list was exercise. "Shouldn't you be–I mean *we* be–finishing the round house?"

"Marion and I had a talk about it last night. We're going to turn the one we've got into a fire pit, and build another one."

Another one? But that wouldn't be done in a day either. Which meant another night of sleeping under the carriage.

"He's full of good ideas that Marion." Joan gave Robyn a wink.

Frustration made her voice come out louder than it should have. "Then put him in charge," Robyn said.

"Hell's teeth!" Joan said, "If Marion were in charge we'd still be back in Loxley weighing up the pros and cons of everything and getting nowhere."

Robyn tried to take it as a compliment, but her mood was too sour. "Yeah, but at least then we'd still have a warm bed for the night."

"Come on," Joan gave her a hug around the shoulders and a too-hard shake. "Let me beat some sense into you."

It wasn't an empty expression. Joan walked Robyn to where a sturdy tree trunk had fallen across the stream many years ago. It was half rotten and wedged into the mud on both sides. Joan fetched two long branches that were rammed in the ground. All set up and waiting for people to come and choose their weapons.

"You are kidding?" Robyn said as she hefted one of the branches into her hands. Someone had cut the side shoots away so that it made a long staff. "It's raining, we don't have a fire, we haven't finished making shelter and you want to play?"

"Not play," Joan twirled her staff like a pro, "I want to fight."

Thwack! Joan spun and slashed her stick through the air. Wrong-footed immediately, Robyn dropped and ducked out the way.

"Get up," Joan demanded.

"Steady on!"

"Get on the bridge." Joan pointed to the tree trunk with her long staff.

"Is your brain clotted?"

Joan's expression was serious. "I said, 'Get. On. The. Bridge.' "

Her friend had officially gone mental. Joan aimed another whack at Robyn. Ready this time, Robyn parried it away.

Another whack. Another defensive block.

Whack, block, thrust, parry. Robyn shuffled on to the tree trunk that Joan had so creatively called a bridge.

"What's got in to you?" Robyn had never seen her friend like this.

Thwack! Robyn ducked, lost her balance, crashed spread-eagled on the trunk. The stream trickled lazily below her, promising an icy bath should she fall in. And no fire as yet to warm herself up.

"We're outlaws now," Joan said.

She must have been talking with Marion.

Joan continued, "We need to look after ourselves and be strong and be ready in a fight."

"We do?"

Thwack! Robyn blocked it with her knuckles. "OW!" Shaking her hand did nothing to ease the pain. "Are you crazy? That really hurt!"

Joan held her staff up, ready for another blow. "Do you think Roger or Maudlin will care if you hurt your hand?"

"They're not here!"

"Not yet maybe, but we need to be ready. On guard!"

"I'm not playing!" Robyn threw her long staff into the stream, where it caught on rocks. Water churned into foam around it.

"This isn't a game." Joan swung her staff like a sword.

Robyn flattened herself against the trunk. The continuing drizzle made it so slippery she lost her footing.

"Saints!" Gravity plummeted her into the icy water. Her screams were louder than the splash. The water, so cold it burned, soaked through everything in a second.

Iced to the core, Robyn struggled out of the river, her clothes miserably heavy. "Are you happy now?"

"You left your longstaff behind."

"You get it then." Robyn stomped off. It was one thing to douse herself in a stream after scaling the walls of a burning tower, quite another to be frozen stiff for no good reason.

Praise heaven! Marion had a fire burning in the incomplete roundhouse. Not a large one by any account, but enough of a small glow.

"You're dripping all over it!" Marion shooed her away.

"C-c-c," Robyn started a sentence that should have been, "Can't get warm enough." She would have hugged the fire to her chest if it would help. Her back teeth clattered together, making words impossible.

"You're soaked!" Marion said.

He'd noticed? "J-J-Jo-" More shivering and rattling teeth. "Joan!" she managed with supreme effort. Rubbing her hands together didn't warm her one bit, but sent droplets hissing onto the meagre fire.

"Careful!"

More splashes hissed onto the flames. She shoved her hands under her armpits to make them warm. It achieved nothing.

"You're freezing. Come here," Marion said.

Robyn couldn't move. Instead, Marion stepped closer and embraced her in a tight hug. "You're made of ice. I shouldn't have let you sleep out last night. I'm so sorry."

"N-n-no-" She couldn't get anything out. She wanted to say, "It's not your fault, Joan did this," but the freezing tremors took hold. When he kissed her on the forehead, his lips were hotter than a branding iron.

"River!" The word flew out like a curse, but at least it was a whole word and maybe Marion could put the pieces together.

"Yes, I can see that you must have fallen in. You'll never get warm if you stay in these." Marion broke their embrace, pulled his tunic off over his head and offered it to her. "Get your wet gear off and put this on."

He stood there in his threadbare undershirt, leaving very little to the imagination. Which made Robyn realise how dangerously cold she had to be, if she couldn't feel any heat in her cheeks at all.

Too frozen to be embarrassed, Robyn dragged at her hooded tunic. Too wet and heavy; her arms too weak. Marion stepped in and finished the job, *shlucking* the fabric away from her goose bump-covered skin. She wrapped her arms around her torso as the air swirled around her bare skin. Not from shame or trying to cover herself, but in a desperate attempt to keep warm. Marion slotted his tunic over her, wrapping the sleeves forward to tie her in to the fabric.

Joan walked into the round house. Marion and Joan talked, but their words became a mash of sounds swirling around her. All she cared about was getting warm. Marion held her tightly in his arms, rubbing her back fiercely to get some heat into her body.

At some point she passed out, because the next moment she

woke in a messy pile of limbs on the ground, Marion holding her steady and rubbing heat into her arms and back. He kept kissing her on the forehead as well, his lips a welcome hot-spot.

Oh, wait a minute. It wasn't Marion. He was cuddling her from behind. The lips on her forehead belonged to her mother.

"She's getting warmer," Eleanor said.

Marion barked more orders. "Joan, bring more wood for the fire."

"But everything's wet?" She complained.

"Then back the carriage in here and we'll burn that!"

More shouting; then everything went woozy and Robyn passed out again. Then she woke again, tucked up in a tight ball, knees under her chin. Marion was still wrapped around her, rubbing her limbs to get warm. A fresh bout of shivers rattled her bones.

"The fire's bright and hot now," Marion murmured into her ear.

Her legs were bare. Getting her bearings, she eyeballed her tunic and frock skirt hooked over the branches on the walls, dripping puddles onto the floor. Marion guided her feet towards the coals. A moment later, her toes felt like they were on fire.

At least her feet were finally warm. Ouch! Too warm.

"Careful! You want to thaw out slowly. Too much and you'll blister," Eleanor said.

Wiping her blurry eyes, Robyn noticed everyone gathered around her, the same worried expression on their faces.

"I'm so sorry for what happened," Joan said. "I just wanted us to be fighting fit. You know? Ready for anything."

"I know. It's OK Joan." It came out in a whisper. Robyn was grateful she could make sentences again.

"I should have at least let you wake up and have breakfast though," Joan said.

In a whisper, Robyn said, "Roger and Maudlin wouldn't."

An uncomfortable silence descended. Marion kept rubbing Robyn's back, but instead of the fierce intensity of before, it had slowed to something more like a caress.

"You're right," he said. "We need to be ready for anything."

They all nodded. At which point Robyn noticed someone missing. "Where's Ellen?"

"Here I am," she said bringing a cloth sack with her. A cloth sack that moved and wriggled. "Hope you all like shellfish." Confused faces abounded as Ellen put the sack on the ground to reveal her catch. "Snappy little biters they are, but if you grab them by the back here, see, they can't get you."

"What are they?" Marion said.

They had a strange, greenish grey colour about them, and they wore a suit of armour.

"Freshwater crayfish!" Ellen beamed as if she'd produced a bag of gold. "All the meat is in the tail, and the claws, but you cook the heads as well to make soup and it's so lush."

Mother Eleanor leaned forward to take a closer look, then leapt back as one of them snapped its enormous claw at her. "They look like something out of a nightmare!"

Ellen looked around. "Well? Who's going to help me?"

Stunned silence. Ellen put her hands on her hips. "If I have to do it all myself, I'll eat it all too."

"Those monsters came out of the river?" Eleanor asked.

"Yep."

"Proves my point. Rivers and humans shouldn't mix. Robyn, let this be a lesson to you. Not only will they try and freeze you to death, but they're full of demons that will flay you alive."

"Mother Eleanor, thank you for volunteering." Ellen said, roping her in to helping with food preparation. "Now, you hold the blade steady like this and bring it down hard here, in one go. That chops the tail off in one hit. The tail's the bit we're going to eat."

Nobody interrupted as Ellen gave her cookery demonstration. The pointy heads with their bobble-eyes went into the pot, the claws and tails put aside for now.

Once the water in the pot began to bubble, the shells changed colour from their mottled grey to bright red.

"What witchcraft is this?" Eleanor asked.

"They look like devil spawn but they taste like heaven," Ellen said.

Soon the aromas filling the little round house set everyone's tummies to gurgling.

What with the bad night's sleep, the fight with Joan and subsequent near death from freezing, Robyn could have eaten one of those monsters, snappy claws and all. Hot soupy smells of roasted nuts and butter teased her senses. All from one little armoured creature that looked like it had crawled from the bowels of hell.

Ellen strained the soup through the bag to get the shell and grit out, then it was time to add the chunks of tail and claw meat.

"Make sure you take the vein out," Ellen said. "I won't lie to you, this is the worst part. The vein is the . . . um . . . food tube."

"Urgh," everyone said as they sliced at the tail meat with their thumbnails and flicked out the dark vein of grit. It was fiddly and frustrating and took forever. Every meal takes forever when you're starving.

Stomach folding in on itself with hunger, the moment it was ready, Robyn had her bowl out.

It was so delicious she couldn't speak.

"It's good, isn't it?" Ellen said.

"Good is an insult," Madge said as she slurped at hers. "This is a dream in a bowl."

"Is there any more?" Georgia asked as she emptied her serve.

"Sorry, that's all there is. But if I set the sack again, we can catch more tomorrow. Plenty more where they came from."

Everyone agreed they would catch more of these devil-creatures, as often as they could.

"You did well to pick this spot," Robyn murmured to Marion.

"Thanks." He gave her a kiss on the cheek.

Everyone saw his kiss and a chorus of "woo" filled the air.

Hot blushes of embarrassment roared up Robyn's neck and spread over her face. It was suddenly too warm in here.

"Your clothes will be dry soon, love," Eleanor said. "Then you can give Marion his tunic back."

Earlier, she'd nearly died of cold. Now she might die of red-hot embarrassment as every gaze fell upon her. Marion had seen her as good as naked and now everyone knew she was wearing his clothes. But it had been an emergency, hadn't it? It wasn't as if she'd had a choice about taking her drenched clothes off.

Far too many eyes were looking at her, leaping to conclusions. Or maybe they simply knew where this was all leading and she was the one protesting too much? Whatever the case, Marion deserved her thanks. She'd been half frozen to death and he'd known exactly what to do. Who cared if everyone was watching? Madge and Wilfred didn't care who saw their affection.

"Thank you," Robyn gave him a gentle kiss on the cheek. It didn't feel like enough so she pulled back and added, "For everything."

His voice low, Marion said, "I was so worried."

Ellen said in a too-loud voice, "Best take these scraps out. We'll use the shells and heads as bait for the next lot."

Some shuffling nearby and movement in the side of her vision told Robyn they'd get some privacy. Some much-needed privacy.

Ears flapping for the sound of everyone leaving them alone, she heard Georgia say, "The soup was amazing."

To which Ellen then said, "I won't lie to you, it's even better with a dollop of cream in it."

Robyn cursed.

"What?" Marion was all confusion.

"That Ellen. She's got them all eating out the palm of her hand."

Marion shrugged. "Yesterday you were complaining that she was one more mouth to feed. Now she's proved how useful she is you don't like her again?"

Robyn folded her arms across her chest. "Come on, 'cream'? That's no accident. She knows mother wants to get Bella back."

Silence for a short while, then Marion tilted her face back to him. "Why are we talking when we could be kissing?"

Wait, what? Kissing?

Marion leaned in and planted a kiss straight onto her mouth. Robyn's eyebrows shot up so high they nearly flew off her face. The pressure of his lips on hers was simply divine. Firm but yielding, warm and wonderful and a little bit thrilling.

Make that a lot thrilling.

"I was so worried about you," he said as he pulled back.

Her tightly held arms unfurled themselves. Strange new feelings took hold. She knew she needed to examine them a little more. Perhaps a lot more. "What was that?"

"One of these." He kissed her again. The second kiss was just as bold as the first, their lips fitting together, the whispery whiskers of his top lip skating over her skin.

Shocked by this rapid change in developments, Robyn let Marion take charge. But only for a moment, only until she worked out the right kind of response. Which was to kiss him back just as firmly as he had kissed her. Except soon after starting what should have been an exploration . . . it felt more like capitulation.

In panic, she pulled back, her breath coming in short bursts of shock. Marion looked different all of a sudden. An unchecked smile spread over his face. Half expecting to hear something self-congratulatory like, "That shut you up," the shocks kept coming when Marion grinned and said, "That was awesome!"

Mesmerized, Robyn touched her fingers to her lips, wondering if this were really happening. The dark centres of Marion's eyes grew large, even though it wasn't anytime near dusk.

This kissing thing. Was it always so . . . magnificent? Curiosity got the better of her and she leaned in for another shot at it. Instinct guided her hand to anchor itself on his shoulder as their lips came together. She felt his strong muscles bunch under her hand, through his thin undershirt. How good would it feel to touch his bare skin? On its own volition, her palm moved northwards to caress his neck and hold him to her. When her fingertips came across a pulse point, she found his heart beating almost as fast as her own.

In response, his arms closed around her waist, locking their bodies together, their chests pressing closer with each shaky intake of breath.

Something flipped in her tummy. Something tentative and unsure of itself. Something that would take a serious amount of kissing to fully investigate. Robyn applied herself to the investigation. She was nothing if not thorough.

Mother Eleanor's voice rang through the air. "I'll just go and check to see if Robyn's clothes are dry."

Reluctantly, Robyn pulled away just as her mother walked in. The woman was humming far too loudly, pretending she had no idea what had been going on in here. "Wasn't that meal delicious Robyn?" Eleanor asked.

"Yes it was."

Robyn and Marion's foreheads were still touching.

"It might be nice to have it with a little cream. Oh good, this is nearly dry. Perhaps only a few more minutes and it will be done. I have Joan fetching more wood for the fire."

The whole time she spoke, Eleanor didn't make eye contact. Then she left the round house and called out to Joan to collect more wood.

Robyn couldn't shut off the nagging voice of warning in her head. "I don't trust Ellen. Even if we managed to get cream, next time it will be something that needs a little butter. After that it will be milk. Before you know it we'll be heading straight into Sheffield to liberate the cow."

A heavy sigh from Marion. "Straight into a trap, yeah?"

"Yeah."

Her rubbed her back. "You're so smart, that's why–" he suddenly coughed, spluttered and pulled back, covering his face. "– Damn smoky fire." More spluttering.

The fire belched smoke, so they shuffled away from the fire. The break in the kissing brought reality intruding back.

"Joan's right, you know," Robyn said.

"About?"

"About the fact we need to be ready, at all times. Roger could be back any time. People could be travelling the Kings Road north and south and see us. Other outlaws could raid our camp."

"As long as getting ready doesn't involve freezing to death," he stroked her face. "I was so worried about you."

"Thank you for unfreezing me," She kissed him again and gave him the best hug she could manage in her exhausted state.

Marion held Robyn's hand to steady her as they ventured out. The rain had slowed to swirling drizzle. Joan and Georgia were teaching Wilfred and Madge how to fight with long staffs. This time, they were doing it on muddy ground instead of balancing on a tree trunk over a freezing river.

Near that same river were Ellen and Eleanor, weaving thin

branches into a basket shape. "Oh, hello Robyn. You're mother's an excellent weaver. We're making crayfish pots for the next catch."

Their fingers deftly wove the soft twigs around and around, creating a wide-bottomed basket.

"Won't they get out?" Robyn asked.

Ellen grinned. "If we left them like this, they surely would. But look, this is the shape we're going to make them into," she said, pointing to some scratches in the mud. Ellen had drawn a bowl with high sides that tapered inwards at the neck, much like a flagon for storing wine. "Some farmers I used to know showed me how to do this. Because of their armour, crayfish can only bend forward, you see, they can't bend their shells back the other way. They can crawl or swim in, but they can't crawl out again. All we do is set the trap and come back later to see how many we have."

The whole time Marion said nothing, but Robyn had a fair idea of what he was thinking. Ellen was making herself useful. Very useful. And she was being so friendly about it. How could they think badly of her when she was being so nice to them?

And cooking the most delicious food they'd ever had.

Trouble was, the longer Ellen stayed with them, the more she'd become an integral part of the group. The more everyone would rely on her skills. The harder it would be to know whether they could really trust her or not.

CHAPTER 12

*I*gnoring the fact they had become outlaws and that Roger–if not Lady Maudlin–would come hunting for them any day now, Robyn looked around their camp and felt a strange sense of comfort with her new life.

Possibly even acceptance.

Since they'd set up camp, Marion had hacked a hole through the top of the round house roof, to act as a chimney and suck the smoke away. He knew what he was doing with fire, that lad. More than a few times Robyn caught herself watching him work, watching the way his muscles flexed and his skin glowed with perspiration. The way the light drizzle of rain coated his skin to gleaming.

After breakfast, Joan would lead them in battle training to get them ready for anything. Robyn taught everyone how to fire a bow, even though they only had one. This was just in case she didn't have it, someone else could grab it and make use of it.

Mother Eleanor and Ellen caught fish, both the regular and cray kind, and made the most delicious stews to keep their bellies full.

Georgia, Will and Madge built a ramshackle stable between some trees, to give the horses them a little shelter from the rain. For the times when the rain fell vertically. They had no defences for the horizontal rain. That was the worst, it got into everything and brought nothing but misery.

Not that Robyn could truly relax. Her mind kept swirling like the drizzle as she recognised problem upon problem. The freezing water she'd fallen into had proven just how close they were to winter. Surely their food would run out as the river iced over?

They might be able to stay in the Shire Wood for another couple of weeks at the most, but they'd need proper warmth and shelter soon. Littleton was out of the question, because Roger and his men had burned the roofs off. There weren't many options back in Loxley either.

They could try for Nottingham, but none of them had ever been there before. Would they receive any kind of welcome there?

If they went back to Sheffield, they knew their way around, but they also knew they'd be hunted and hounded out. Or strung up.

Could they stay in the Shire Wood, through a proper winter? It hadn't snowed . . . yet. Then what? Huddle together in the round house and burn everything they had to keep warm and then . . . and then? Would they starve? Would the horses survive?

Looking at the faces around her, Robyn didn't see her worries pressing down on anyone else's shoulders. Did they think ahead about winter's cold teeth on their necks?

Or were they leaving everything for Robyn to sort out?

"What's wrong?" Marion said, appearing by her side.

"Oh! Didn't see you there," she said, patting her chest to settle her heart down.

He'd run his fingers roughly through his hair and it looked so tousled and . . . interesting. "Can we talk for a bit?" He said, tilting his head, "Away from this lot?"

"Of course," she said without hesitation.

A quick glance showed Robyn the rest of their "lot" were watching Joan and Madge in a long staff battle.

"This way," Marion's voice was low and conspiratorial.

Robyn's heart tripped when Marion wrapped his hand in hers. Both their hands were work-worn and cold, but the effect of them coming together warmed her from the inside. A sneaky little voice in her head said they were skiving off for some kisses. Or at the very least, some alone time. Excellent! They crossed the tree-trunk bridge and came to a clearing on the other side of the river.

Marion turned to Robyn and placed his finger over his lips in the universal "shushing" motion. He had a surprise for her? How lovely!

Quieter than mice, they came to the edge of a clearing to find . . .

Saints!

Ellen. And on her shoulder sat a jackdaw. A glossy, small crow just like the one that clung to Maudlin.

Robyn's spirit slumped. No sound came out of her, but inside her head she heard ringing bells of doom. The jackdaw proved that Ellen was still in communication with Maudlin.

Worse, she and Marion wouldn't be having a kissing session.

Silently they crept back to the training ground where Madge, by some miracle, was making improvements and getting in a couple of good offensive shots.

"We'll have to leave again, won't we?" Robyn said as they stayed back a bit, pretending to watch the battle.

"That crow will lead Maudlin right to us," Marion confirmed.

"We could always leave Ellen here."

"Can she hibernate?"

Darn that Marion for being right. A group of them, working together, with enough supplies (which they didn't have anyway) might stand a chance of surviving the winter. But one girl on her own? Not a hope. As much as she hated having to keep Ellen with them, she couldn't live with herself if she abandoned Ellen to the wilderness.

After some more thinks, Robyn said, "Let's dump her back at Sheffield then."

"And then what?"

"I don't know. Stop making me come up with everything!"

"I didn't mean it to come out like that," Marion said.

Ooops, she'd raised her voice and everyone turned to look at them. At this point, Ellen returned from her little hiding spot. Minus the bird, but plus a sack of fish. Robyn had to think fast. "We need to get Bella back, otherwise we won't survive winter."

Mother Eleanor ran toward her and smothered her in kisses. "You're such a good girl."

"Yeah, yeah," Robyn said, fighting off her affection. It didn't feel right to take praise for something she hadn't really meant. They had to ditch Ellen somehow, but they had to make it look like they weren't ditching her. Then they needed to find a safe, warm place for the cold months ahead, and a forest glade wasn't it.

Everyone made their way to the roundhouse, where the fire kept them toasty warm. All eyes turned to Robyn, wanting to know what to do next. That was the bit that got her, right in the solar plexus. They were all looking to her for leadership. Even Marion. Georgia and Mother Eleanor were the elders of the group, but they too had somehow shrugged off the mantle of responsibility and piled it on her shoulders.

And still those eyes looked her way, filled with admiration and–how irritating–hope. Which only added to the sense Robyn would let them down.

Horribly.

Marion gave Robyn a gentle nudge of encouragement.

No words came. Robyn's mind had gone blank.

Giving her a quizzical look, Marion cleared his throat. "We're going back to Sheffield, and we're getting Bella. Any suggestions for how we do this?"

"Bash the guards, kick the gate in and grab the cow," Georgia said.

What it lacked in sophistication it more than made up for in cathartic action. "I like it," Robyn said.

"We can't simply bash our way through, people are bound to get hurt," Madge said, wrapping her arm around Wilfred.

"We could buy her back," Eleanor said.

This was met with nods and murmurs of approval.

Robyn had to disappoint them. "Not to put a dampener on the enthusiasm, but we don't have any coins left to buy her.

"We could trade for her," Ellen said, "I've set the crayfish traps, they'll be crawling with fresh ones by morning."

Robyn tried not to smile too much at Ellen's suggestion. Of course the girl wanted to get back to Sheffield. She had clearly seen which way the wind was blowing—cold and from the north—and knew it was suicide to stay out in the woods for much longer. But they couldn't simply stroll back to the front gates at Sheffield and expect to be let in. It would play directly into Maudlin's hands for them to return and ask to be let in.

It would also save Maudlin from having to send out a search party. Strange that this hadn't happened already.

Heaviness weighed in Robyn's stomach. Perhaps Roger and his men were already on their way? They'd have a fight on their hands, obviously. If he had a lick of sense, Roger would bring reinforcements this time.

"We need to be prepared just in case Roger and his men try and capture us," Marion said as Robyn was formulating the words in her own brain.

"We've been training," Joan said. "Even Madge is getting good."

"Aw, thanks Joan," Madge said.

"No really, you are," Will added. "Plus, you're short so it's easier for you to ram them in the soft bits."

"Maybe the crayfish and one of the horses would make a good trade?" Ellen suggested.

Oh, she was crafty.

Marion piped up. "Would they see that as a fair trade?"

Nice one, Marion. He wasn't dismissing Ellen's argument, just being his normal, 'think everything through to the last degree,' self. It would drive Ellen crazy.

The discussion around the fire continued. During the too-ing and fro-ing, Robyn had to hide her face a few times so the others wouldn't see her smiling so much. The fire belched smoke with each new branch placed on top. It helped hide her laughs with a coughing fit. They were all coughing now, and for a while they stood outside in the fresh air, until the rain picked up again and they huddled back around the fire.

Soon, everyone was sharing ideas about how to get to Sheffield, get the cow, and get out again.

"If we're caught, we'll be thrown in the dungeons," Marion reminded them.

"But the d–" Robyn pulled herself up short and pretended to have another cough. She'd almost revealed what she knew about the dungeons. She knew they weren't empty. Well, they did have one human prisoner down there, and he flapped his hands about like a man with no alms. But the other cells were being used to store Maudlin's ill-gotten gains that Roger and his crew had taxed from all the neighbouring villages. With a bit of luck and some planning–she'd ask Marion about how they should go about that–they wouldn't end up in the dungeons. But they would get those ill-gotten goods out of the dungeons.

"What were you going to say?" Ellen asked, trying–and failing in Robyn's mind–to look innocent.

Quick, think of something. "I was thinking that the dungeons aren't guarded. Well, not anymore." She said. Because they weren't, what with Georgia the ex-turnkey being one of them now. And Wilfred who used to guard the gates. "Will? Georgia? How many guards are left in Sheffield?"

"I don't know," Wilfred said. "I'm sure Godwin is still at the gate."

Georgia shrugged and said, "She may have hired more since our last dust-up."

"This could work for us," Ellen said, revealing her enthusiasm. "Sheffield isn't well guarded. Why don't we simply walk up to the gates, ask to be let in and see what happens?"

"See if we're arrested, you mean," Madge said as she clung to Wilfred.

The fire crackled and popped as they mulled this over.

"We're overlooking one thing," Joan said, "I don't trust Ellen as far as I could throw her. And you shouldn't be trusting her either."

Robyn's stomach sank. Joan was about to blow everything.

"Fair enough," Marion said. "Ellen, I'm sorry, but with your connection to Maudlin, I don't think we can ever fully trust you."

The perfect intercept. Thank you Marion.

"Of course you can trust me!" Ellen protested. "I'm here with you lot! Freezing my tits off when I could be in Sheffield, covered in sheep skins in front of a roaring fire!"

"This fire's pretty good," Marion said.

Robyn heard the defensive tone in his voice and gave his arm a squeeze. "It's a great fire."

"I say we continue this without Maudlin's eyes and ears on us," Joan said as she stood up and held her hand out for Ellen to take. "Come on girl, time to get back in your box."

"Honestly, you're all so unfair!" Ellen protested as Joan lifted her up by one armpit and guided her—with some dragging—to their carriage sleep-out. The carriage stood a few paces from the round house, close enough to be warm, distant enough to prevent it catching fire should the worst happen.

"Please Joan, what do I have to do to earn your trust again? I've been working so hard, catching food and cooking the best meals. I thought you liked me?"

"I do like you," Joan said as she opened the carriage door and shoved Ellen in, "But there's no way I trust you."

"You trust Georgia, and she worked for Maudlin!"

"That's different," Joan said as she pushed Ellen's head back so she'd fit in her box. "Georgia's my mother."

Tears welled in the former-jailers eyes. "I never thought I'd see her again. Not a day went by when I didn't wonder what she looked like. If she was healthy." The tears broke down Georgia's cheeks. "If she was happy."

Over by the carriage, Joan stood by the door, leaning her head into the frame but saying nothing. They could hear Ellen's muffled voice inside, but couldn't make out the words.

Georgia swiped her face with her sleeve and continued. "And now I've taken her from her home parents. They're still in Sheffield. They must be worried sick about her."

Guilt churned Robyn's stomach. She'd completely forgotten about Joan's elderly parents.

"OK, let's not talk too loudly because Ellen can probably over-hear us," Robyn said.

"La la la la la!" Ellen's muffled voice sang out.

"I'm going to tell you what I saw in Sheffield, in the dungeons," Robyn began. She had to trust Wilfred and Georgia at this point. They had to be a cohesive group or they'd fall apart. Trusting them with this information was the fastest way to show them they were all in this together.

Over the course of the next few logs on the fire, Joan joined them and warmed herself up. Robyn told them how Roger and Maudlin were collecting taxes for the Sheriff of Nottingham, but also how they were keeping piles and piles of stuff for themselves. Not just things stolen from Loxley, but from every village within one or two days' ride from Sheffield. All collected under the name of the Sherriff of Nottingham. He'd be the one people cursed during the winter, when he probably had no idea what Roger and Maudlin were up to.

"It's quite the conspiracy, when you think about it," Robyn said. "Roger steals it all but Nottingham gets the blame."

Everyone nodded and looked thoughtful.

"Now," she said, looking around the group, "Let's all put our heads together and make a plan."

Marion put his arm around her shoulder and pulled her in for a kiss on the cheek. "Whatever we decide, I'm with you all the way."

"Me too," Georgia said, reaching into the long pocket on the inside of her tunic. "It's the master key to the dungeons. Should work, unless Maudlin's changed the locks?"

They kept their voices low and conspired into the wee small hours. They would travel to Sheffield, leave Shadow tied up a little way from the gate, then offer to trade Plus One and bag of devilfish for the cow and see where that got them. If they stayed the night in Sheffield, they'd use the key to steal whatever they could carry from the dungeons and make their getaway.

Eventually everyone staggered back to the carriage to sleep. Mother Eleanor made for the undercarriage again but Marion stopped her and guided her to the carriage door instead, offering her his place inside.

From the distance, Robyn couldn't tell what they were talking about, but eventually her mother climbed in.

Instead of heading straight back to the round house, Marion loaded more wood into his arms and brought it back to the fire. He put the pieces to the side to dry out, stacking them neatly as if he had all the time in the world.

Pulling her knees up to her chin, Robyn gazed into the coals.

"Don't get cross," Marion said. "But now that we've made a public plan we've told the others about, we need to have a contingency plan."

"Come on!" Was he serious?

"Shh! Keep you voice down. Your mother has ears like a bat."

Robyn muttered, "I've already planned things, and now you're saying it's not enough?"

"I asked you not to get cross. What happens if we're arrested and thrown in the dungeons for real?"

"We've got the key, we'll get out again."

"And what if they lock us up somewhere else, or if they change the locks in the dungeons?"

Robyn threw her hands up. "I can't think of everything."

He smiled and looked at her with an admiring gaze. "Don't be so hard on yourself. You're doing an amazing job."

"Don't try to butter me up."

"But you are," he kissed her forehead, then her cheek, then he tucked her hair and kissed the spot just under her ear. "You're amazing."

"Oh stop," she only half batted him away. How was a girl supposed to stay cross when he kissed her like that? He cradled her chin and angled her lips his way. "I want to make sure you're safe, and I want to make sure this works. That's why we need to plan for all the different ways this could work out." Then he kissed her and lit a fire inside her.

"Wow," she said as he pulled away. "When you put it like that." She leaned in for another kiss. They wouldn't need the fire to keep warm tonight, they were creating enough heat already.

A commotion broke out in the carriage. Doors slammed, people yelled, somebody charged off into the night.

"She's getting away!" Georgia yelled. The woman took a few steps but was far too slow to do anything. She'd been built for strength, not speed.

A small dark figure scampered off into the shadows.

A heavy sigh took Robyn's breath.

"Ellen?" Marion asked.

"Yep. She's gone. I'd give chase but . . ." Georgia let out a sigh. "No point charging off into the woods in this darkness. She'll go straight back to Sheffield, won't she?"

"Yeah." Defeat leached the strength from Robyn's bones.

"There is an upside?" Marion said.

Robyn looked at him with confusion crinkling her brows, so he replied, "Saves us having to take her."

CHAPTER 13

*R*obyn woke to the sound of fighting. Thwacks with sticks. Groans. Punches. Fists bashing from the inside of the carriage door. She leapt up without thinking and biffed her head on the wheel axle. "Ow!" she rubbed her head and scooted out from under the carriage.

To find Roger of Doncaster and at least a dozen others attacking their Shire Wood camp. Three were pulling down the roundhouse and–total lack of imagination–set it on fire. Another four or five, it was hard to tell with all the movement, took on Joan in the clearing.

With nothing to grab for a weapon, Robyn set upon the one of Joan's attacker, jumping on his back. The attacker flailed at her with his stick, crying out for help. Joan clonked him on the head, causing both of them to fall. Only Robyn got up, the other lay there moaning on the ground. He'd be fine, if sore, in a few hours.

"Where are the others?" Robyn cried out as Joan kept up her defence against the rest of them and Robyn crouched, ready to pounce.

"Locked in the carriage."

"Right then!" Robyn darted to the carriage where a guard stood, the door firmly wedged shut.

"You'll have to go through me, lass," the guard said.

"Fine then." Robyn darted away and heard him laughing behind her. If he thought her a coward, all the better. Avoiding Joan and her three attackers (another had fallen by the wayside with a sick grunt) Robyn grabbed the unburned end of long stick that used to be part of the round house. She headed back to the carriage. Approaching from the non-guarded side, she slipped under the carriage and wriggled forward. She could see the guard's boots and the bottom of his pants. They didn't quite meet, the pants being far too short, exposing a sturdy ankle and healthy crop of curly dark leg-hair.

Perfect.

Robyn held the glowing coals closer and closer to the man's leg. Because of the pants-gap, his cuffs were a long way from the wet ground, and therefore dry. The coals only needed a slight breeze to glow a satisfying orange, and his leg hairs and pants were alight!

"Ahhhhhh!" The man screamed and leapt away from the heat, battering at his smouldering leg.

Seizing her chance, Robyn dashed out from underneath, then pulled with all her might at the carriage door, where the rest of her friends were locked inside. Marion and Will leapt out first, taking on Roger's men. With a war cry, Georgia scrambled for fresh air, calling for Joan. Mother Eleanor and Madge sat inside.

Madge looked at Robyn with innocent eyes and pleaded, "Can we stay in here please?"

"Fair enough." Robyn shut the door closed and joined in the fray.

In all the plans they'd made, they hadn't planned on an ambush. But it made perfect sense that Roger would come for them. He'd want to catch them by surprise, and that's exactly what he'd done.

The round house lay in smouldering splinters. Robyn grabbed one of the support beams that now lay on the ground and used it as a long staff to defend herself from two attackers who appeared out of nowhere. They were relentless and strong. Meanwhile Joan and Georgia were laying waste to their attackers. Any moment now they'd come and give her a little support.

Any moment.

Now would be a good time to "Ow!" her attacker got her in the leg and she hobbled backwards.

This guy wasn't going to give up. With a brutal lurch, Robyn got him in the stomach, then she stumbled on her bad leg back to the safety of the carriage.

She pulled the door open and Mother Eleanor sat there with Robyn's bow and arrow. "Will this help?"

"Yes it will!"

She grabbed the quiver full of arrows and slipped it over her shoulder, then with the bow over her other shoulder, she scrambled onto the top of the wagon.

"Everybody stop!"

Nobody wanted to stop.

"I said stop!" An arrow whizzed through the air, narrowly missing a man attacking Marion with a long staff.

Robyn pulled another arrow into position. "Now put down your weapons or the next will hit true!"

Slowly, they did what she said, laying down whatever they were using and all facing Robyn. From here she could count how many there were on both sides. Her friends were still standing, which was excellent. She was sure there should be some of Roger's men lying passed out on the ground, but there was a dozen, no, fourteen of them. Not counting Roger, the target of her next arrow. The tight string dug into her finger pads. Weak sunlight glinted off his sweaty forehead. She moved her sights onto other men and some women standing closest to Roger. Nice of him not to discriminate in his choice of hench-staff. "Who here is willing to die for Roger of Doncaster, the tax collector? Step forward now and meet the almighty!" As she'd hoped, nobody moved forward.

"Good!" She said, impressed with how persuasive a bow and arrow could be. She returned her sights to Roger. "Doncaster! Gather your brutes and get back to Sheffield where you belong, cowering behind Maudlin's skirts!"

Joan, Georgia, Marion and Will all laughed.

Will gave his closest attacker a smack over the side of the head. "That's for making Madge cry," he said.

"Will, behave yourself!" Robyn warned. "We might be outlaws but we treat people with respect. Now say sorry!"

"What?" Will protested.

"Go on!" Robyn aimed her arrow at Will for good measure.

"I'm sorry," he said quickly.

"Good." Robyn resumed her aim at Roger's torso. He wore thick padding but not armour. Would the arrow pierce it? If she struck it hard enough it could. "Go on Roger, get back to Sheffield before I really lose my temper."

Shaking his head in defeat, Roger walked to the edge of the clearing where he'd left his horse near a tree. "This is only a reprieve, hoodlum. You will get yours!"

Robyn let the arrow loose. It pierced Roger's hat and nailed it into a tree behind him. Roger spurred his horse away from the clearing. Saints! She'd meant to get him in the shoulder. She hadn't dared aim any lower lest it hit the horse.

She turned and faced the rest of the men and women. "You're free to join us and become outlaws in the Shire Wood, or return to Sheffield. I won't hold a grudge against you whichever you choose.

They looked around at their options. Some of them shook hands with Robyn's friends, muttering things like. "No harm done."

"Rather decent."

"All things considered."

"Family things, you'd understand."

"Best get back."

They too headed towards the edge of the clearing and the nearby Kings Road that would take them back to Sheffield. Exhausted from the confrontation, Robyn scrambled down and found herself in Marion's arms.

"You were amazing!"

Everyone wanted to hug Robyn and pat her on the back. It was suffocatingly wonderful. They'd won. For now.

"OK everyone, let's have breakfast and get ourselves ready to take on Sheffield!" Marion said.

Buoyed by their victory, they cheered. Robyn felt sick to her boots. Her body shook from adrenaline racing through it. They'd just taken on Roger's band of misfits and won. Which was brilliant.

But how were they going to win against a whole castle?

~

TIRED FROM THEIR BATTLE, the walk to Sheffield was mercifully dull. Except for the part where they jumped at shadows and wore themselves out from constantly watching out for attacks. Which never came.

Here, their plans became stuck. Not from the mud in the road but by Godwin at the recently repaired gate. The hunched-over man with a corkscrew for a spine insisted on asking for their papers. Of which they had none. Did anybody have papers in these parts? Paper sounded expensive.

Godwin looked at them with a sneer and said, "Can't let you in if you don't have papers."

"Seriously? Godwin, do you want a matching lump on the other side of your head?" Robyn asked.

"Easy," Marion said.

"I don't make the rules," Godwin said.

Could they quickly make a plan to clonk Godwin over the head?

For a moment Godwin eyed the horse, Plus One. They'd left Shadow munching on the last of their oats a little further down the road.

"Do you have proof you own that horse?" Godwin asked.

"Do you have proof you're allowed to stop people at the gate?" Robyn shot back.

"As a matter of fact, I do." Despite his gnarled frame, he moved quickly and tugged at the long rope, ringing the warning bell.

"I've just thought of something," Marion said as he grabbed Plus One's reins from Robyn. "What if we split up?"

"Why would we split up? That's a crazy idea."

The enormous gates creaked open and there, standing on the other side, was Roger of Doncaster and his motley assortment of tax collectors-slash-thieves.

"Saints!" Robyn shouted.

"Everyone split up!" Marion yelled as he leapt to the ground.

Roger's mob charged forward. Chaos broke out. Robyn ran underneath the horse and out the other side. Roger grabbed for her tunic but she slipped away.

"Hello!" Ellen said with a wave from the gates.

Fury filling her veins, Robyn ran straight for Ellen to knock her to the ground. Ellen merely locked her stance and met Robyn with equal force. The two thumped into each other with a sickening crunch, sending them staggering backwards.

Head swimming, Robyn jumped to her feet and ran. She didn't even know what direction she ran in, she simply barrelled into Sheffield and hoped to find somewhere to hide. Something dragged at her throat, suddenly her feet left the ground. It was Ellen, holding the neck of Robyn's tunic firmly in her fist.

"Maudlin is really keen to see you," Ellen said.

Robyn would have said something particularly cutting, except her throat was closed over. The rest of the gang ran off in all directions.

Roger couldn't get all of them, could he? *Please let them get away.*

Were they getting away? Robyn twisted from Ellen's grasp. Ow! Godwin stepped in her path and clonked her in the side. For a twisted old man, he sure was fast with the whacking. Tears sprang, it hurt so much! Robyn cried out, just as Godwin aimed another blow her way. Everything went a bit wonky and dark.

When she woke, Robyn found herself locked in a small room with a narrow window. It wasn't the dungeon, it had been a cold place made with blocks of stone. This place felt warmer, less draughty. If she weren't being held prisoner, she might almost call it a comfortable place to retire. Not that she was going to get comfortable. She was going to get out.

There was a narrow window on one wall, so she angled her shoulders in alignment with the window frame and pushed herself through. Her head stuck against the timber. If she kept pushing through, she'd probably rip her ears off. Defeated, she pulled herself back into the room, earning splinters in the side of her head. A head that was already sore and a little wonky from the bashing she earned from Godwin. She had seriously paid the price for underestimating the crooked old man.

Gingerly, she rubbed her fingers over her skin and tried to flick the tiny shards of wood out of her skin. Ow, ow, ow! She kept touching her face and pushing and prodding the skin until at last one of them came free. It left a stinging sensation, but at least it was out.

Stuck in the room for who knew how long, Robyn squeezed the last of her splinters away and took a seat on the one chair in the room. It had a high timber back that was surprisingly comfortable. There wasn't a bed, but there was a table, and its surface was polished to a soft shine. No chance of splinters, she'd shove it in the corner and use it to sleep on later.

One wall featured a shelf filled with books. There had to be at least twenty of them. All leather-bound. She picked one up, opened the pages and had a flick through. One after another, Robyn opened the books. None of them had pictures apart from the tangled illustration on the first page of each chapter. The design was stunning. Such a shame she couldn't read.

Maybe, when all this was over, Marion might teach her how?

The books felt so good in her hands. They had the most deliciously earthy smell to them. While she still had nothing to do and who knew how much time to fill before anyone came for her, she sat in the chair and flicked through the pages. The text swam in front of her eyes, but it felt nice sitting and pretending.

Footsteps grew closer and the door suddenly flung open. Maudlin stood there with a satisfied look on her face and a jackdaw on her shoulder. "It's all right. I'm not going to ask you any tricky questions."

Stones churned in Robyn's stomach. So much for all their plans. "We came back to trade a horse and some fish in exchange for the cow. We just want our cow back and we'll leave."

Maudlin sighed. "You know that's not possible."

"What are you going to do with me then?"

"I'm not sure yet," Maudlin cocked her head to one side and the bird did the same. "Marion's already told me everything."

Marion had been captured? When? What had Marion told her? Trying–and failing–to keep the wobble out of her voice, she said, "We don't have any secrets."

"You misunderstand me. When I say 'there's no need to talk,' I mean stay quiet." Two pairs of pitch black eyes bore down on her.

That little raven on her shoulder. Never in her life had Robyn wished harm to another animal, but the urge to rip every feather from its body while it yet lived was so strong her fingers curled.

"That's better," Maudlin said at Robyn's silence. "I like it when you behave. Makes things run smoother."

Behave? Forget it. "Where's my mother?"

A slick smile broke Maudlin's face. "Your mother has her beloved bovine. She is utterly content and will remain in Sheffield through the winter. Strange woman that, putting a cow ahead of her own daughter's welfare."

The words ate like acid. "You're just trying to upset me."

"I don't have to try." Maudlin made a strange snort before she went on, "I thought my family was horrid, praying all those years for a boy that never came. But your lot? Fancy putting a beast of burden ahead of your own flesh and blood."

"You're just saying that to make me upset. You think I'll cry and say things I'll regret."

Another of those cold smiles. "I do. I get a thrill from watching people break down. I find after they fall to bits, they're only too happy to be reassembled. I can't wait to take you apart and put you back together again."

Barely a third of what she said made sense to Robyn. Maybe Marion had been right with his incessant planning. Robyn should have planned for being captured. Considering how badly things were going for them, she should have considered the worst-case scenario. Cold dread grew in her belly. Being captured wasn't the worst thing. She didn't want to think about the absolute worst thing right now.

"We can stay here for as long as it takes," Maudlin said.

As long as what takes? Robyn wanted to know, but she figured she may as well take Maudlin's earlier advice and stay quiet for a while.

"I have your friends here in Sheffield, working for me. They'd be stupid to be anywhere else at this time of year. And of course there's Marion. I can see why you'd do anything for him."

Robyn's eyes widened at Marion's name, only to see Maudlin fanning herself with her hand. "Oh yes. He's exactly what a lady needs to keep her warm on a cold winter's night."

Robyn nearly threw up.

"Same time tomorrow then?" Maudlin added a cackle for good measure. "Don't get up, I'll see myself out. Oh, and one more thing. I've sent a message to the Earl of Derby. He'll be so pleased I found the outlaws who stole his carriages and horses, although he'll be none too happy with the condition they're in." With that, she swept out.

Saints! Robyn ran for the door and pulled at it, but Maudlin must have locked it from the other side. "Oh yeah? Is that the Sheriff of Nottingham, the one you're supposed to give all your taxes to? I bet he can't wait to find out—"

The door swung open so fast Robyn fell onto her bottom. Maudlin's blotched face towered over hers. "Just you try, peasant. You say one word about that and you'll be worm food faster than you can blink!" The woman slammed the door behind her.

Instead of panicking, Robyn couldn't help smiling. Maudlin was rattled, and Robyn had done the rattling. If the Earl of Derby arrived, Robyn could show him Maudlin's betrayal. As long as she could get to him, which would take a little cunning and a lot of planning.

Not that she had a clue how she'd do that. In their double planning (or was it triple planning?) she and Marion had thought they might be split up or locked up, but they'd thought it would be in the dungeons, the ones Georgia's key would open.

She hadn't planned on being up here. She wasn't even sure how 'up' she was, so she went to the narrow window again and gently pressed her face closer. Not too close, she didn't want splinters again. But enough to see she was at eye level with high tree branches, and not the ground. Even if she could break the window edges, how would she climb down? Which brought Robyn to the realization that no matter how much Marion loved making plans, sometimes you simply had to deal with the situation as it developed.

Tiredness took over. The wooden table would be the most comfortable place to sleep. Robyn grabbed a couple of leather-clad books to support her head and she lay down. Which is when she found another splinter. She sat up, curled her knees under her chin and leaned against the wall. Enough to hold her in a steady position and not agitate the embedded splinter. The injury made her head throb, even though she knew the shards of wood had to be tiny wee things.

Maudlin is not going to get to me. She promised herself.

No way.

I will not let her upset me one bit.

That crow though . . .

CHAPTER 14

*B*y morning, Maudlin came back, carrying a tray of hot porridge and a tankard of something delicious, with steam rising from it. The little crow sat on her shoulder, like a second pair of eyes, never taking its gaze from Robyn. Being the confusing person she was, Maudlin placed the tray on the floor instead of on the table. Robyn's mouth watered in response.

"Doing a little reading were you?" Maudlin reached for the books on the table and replaced them on the shelf.

All things considered, Robyn hadn't slept too badly. The table was as uncomfortable as the cold ground under the carriage, but at least she didn't clonk her head when she sat up. Involuntarily, she licked her lips at the sight of food.

"Are you hungry?" Maudlin mocked her. "You're lucky there was any porridge to spare. We have so many more people seeking shelter with us. We don't have much to see us through winter," her eyes narrowed, "as somebody stole the bags of oats we had." Then her tone changed to something almost pleasant. "The mug is hot cider. Would you like some?"

"Yes." She'd be able to think better on a full stomach and a drink. Whatever hot cider was. A sarcastic response nearly leapt out as she noticed there was no spoon. She'd make do then, picking up the bowl with one hand and shovelling the porridge in with her fingers.

Maudlin tutted and said, "Such terrible table manners. Any wonder your mother prefers the cow."

Tease me all you want, abuse me, I don't care. Who had time to speak when the hot porridge warmed her from within? It was thick and filling and creamy and quite simply the best meal she'd had in ages, after Ellen's armoured fish.

"Would you like more?" Maudlin asked.

"Is there?"

"No there is not."

She was toying with her, trying to make her angry. But the warm oats in Robyn's belly chased the unease away. She sipped the tankard of hot cider. It tasted like heaven. The rich smell of apples, the warmth of the liquid, the soft bubbles on her tongue . . . it nearly brought her undone. Slurp, slurp, she sucked it in.

"My, my," Maudlin said, "Who would have thought you'd be so entertaining?"

Robyn gave up trying to work out what Maudlin was trying to achieve and drained her tankard of cider. A burp leapt out. Robyn giggled. Maybe it was the food, most likely it was the cider, but she curled up on the floor and fell asleep, not caring if Maudlin was there or not.

SOMEBODY NUDGED HER AWAKE. It was Maudlin. Or, more accurately, Maudlin's booted foot. And she was kicking rather than nudging. Muscles burned as Robyn righted herself. The porridge she'd eaten had migrated into her brain.

"The Earl of Derby's on his way." That manic gleam in her eye—and the jackdaw's—was back. "Tell me everything, and I might be able to convince him to spare you."

Confused and barely awake, Robyn's mouth filled with ash as she spoke. "What?"

"Pardon!" Maudlin corrected her.

"Pardon?" Robyn croaked. Seriously, not a drop of moisture to spare, she couldn't even lick her lips. And her eyes were so crusted with gunk she could barely open them properly.

With one firm finger, Maudlin lifted Robyn's chin to speak directly to her. "I said if you tell me everything, I might convince the Earl to spare your miserable life."

"Why?" Robyn croaked.

"Why would I spare you?"

Not that. "Why . . . does Derby want me?"

Smugness made the edge of Maudlin's mouth curl upwards. "You're so naive. Roger was on the King's official business, on behalf of Derby. You interfered with that, which is treason."

Confusion swirled inside her. She didn't even know what treason was, but it sounded horrible. "I didn't mean it."

"That's a good start. Now, why don't we get you a nice warm bath and some clean clothes and you can tell me everything."

It all sounded so . . . reasonable . . . and a warm bath as well? Saints! There had to be something in that cider because her priorities were all out of whack. She could die happy if she had a warm bath.

"They will hang you tomorrow," Maudlin said as she led Robyn to a room where a steaming, cloth-lined tub sat in the centre.

"Yeah . . ." Distracted by the inviting bath, Robyn pulled her tunic off her head, her muscles as stiff as the boards she'd slept on. Robyn pushed her skirt down to climb in.

"Not worried about modesty, are you?"

"Huh?" Robyn stepped into the tub. Her feet, frozen from the onset of winter and no shoes, fairly boiled as she stepped in. She sank her cold body into the hot water, then shoved her feet out the top to give them a reprieve.

With the same tone that she might use to say, "It's looking like rain," Maudlin said, "Marion was the same."

"What?" Robyn's head whipped around to face Maudlin through the fog of the bath. She had to wave her hands about to clear it.

"Good, you're listening," Maudlin said, pulling up a stool and sitting herself down.

From behind a tapestry, a maid appeared and took Robyn's

dirty clothing away. Which meant she was trapped in the bath with no clothes to dress herself in, and Maudlin appeared to have no intention of leaving.

Enveloped in hot water, Robyn's mind turned to slurry. Her dry throat told her to drink, so she slid further into the bath, until the hot water seeped over her chin. She slurped a little. The water tasted strange and brackish. A strong urge to sleep took hold so she closed her eyes to give them a rest.

"Don't fall asleep in the tub, you'll drown," Maudlin said, "Marion nearly did. I had to drag him out."

Had Marion been in this very tub? The water looked far too clear to be second-hand. If Marion had been in this tub, and Maudlin had sat nearby . . . did that mean she'd seen him . . . as in, *seen him*? Jealousy spiked. "Did you steal his clothes as well?"

"Careful, you're beginning to sound ungrateful. But yes, he too had his first bath in years. Climbed in the colour of mud, came out like a newborn. Well," she cleared her throat, "a little more developed than a newborn. I can see why you fancy him." Maudlin fanned her face with her hand.

Heat roared through Robyn and not because of the bath. How unfair that Lady Maudlin should see more of Marion than she had! Honestly, it was a wonder she didn't sink under the water there and then. Robyn slapped her face to focus on the here and now. When that didn't work, she dunked her head under, swishing her hair in the water. Gingerly she touched her head where the splinters were. Maybe the water would soften her skin and push the last one out?

When Robyn broke through the water's surface again, Maudlin said, "What are we going to do with you?"

Too busy enjoying the bath, Robyn ignored Maudlin. It was so nice and warm and blissful. Her aching muscles softened. Another few minutes and she'd feel brand new and ready to face the world. Which was when something Maudling had said earlier popped into Robyn's head. "You're going to hand me over to the Earl of Derby. So he can hang me?"

"Let's have a chat about that, shall we?" Maudlin said.

"You know that I know you're hiding all that loot in the dungeons. They're taxes you're supposed to hand over to The Earl.

The way I see it, that's *tree-sums*. You might have to kill me before the Earl gets here, to stop me telling him what I know."

"It's pronounced *tree-zun* dear, and I am completely in the clear. No fool would send everything to The Earl in the one carriage. There's too great a risk of losing it to outlaws. In fact, the Earl will be grateful that I'm storing the taxes so conscientiously and I've capture so many outlaws. I've made Sheffield safer."

Utterly cornered, so to speak, Robyn tried to think

Maudlin made a moue with her lips, then said, "Poor girl, you were so sure of yourself a minute ago."

That was the truth. Nothing Robyn said had made a dent in the woman's confidence. Was this how Maudlin converted Ellen to her side? A night in isolation, followed by a hearty breakfast and cider then a steaming bath chaser?

Maudlin smiled so much it reached her eyes and made triangle creases in her skin. The jackdaw on her shoulder tucked its head under a wing and slept. "Robyn dear, I want you to be honest, what do you think me?"

Without thinking, Robyn said, "I think you're weird."

"Weird is good."

Laughter barked from Robyn. She'd expected Maudlin to be angry at the insult, instead she'd taken it as a compliment.

"We live in interesting times," Maudlin said. "One must adapt to changes or be lost to history. Who remembers the old Kings of the Angles and Saxons anymore? Gone as swift as a river carries a teardrop to the sea. My forebears were gifted Sheffield for their loyalty to the King. My grandfather bequeathed it to me. I inherited only because he had no sons or grandsons to name. How lucky am I to be considered a slightly better option than the estate returning to the crown?" Maudlin looked away. Was she crying? Surely not.

"Do you know what else? If I marry, all my family property, including Sheffield, is automatically transferred to my husband's ownership. If I have no sons, he could hand everything upon his death to his nephews or brothers or cousins. That is hardly fair, is it?"

Confusion swirled like rising bath mist. "I'm sorry Maudlin, but all that bequeathing stuff is over my head."

"Of course. You are merely a peasant. What would you know of property or inheritance?"

"Is there a point to this?"

"You are rude!" Maudlin said.

"Sorry."

Looking downcast, Maudlin said in a soft voice, "You are rude, but you are also right. I am weird, and I'm proud of it. You see, I have made choices in this life, choices which allow me to stay in control of my circumstances. I cannot marry, that would cede all power to my husband. I mislike that. I want to retain control of Sheffield; therefore I must not marry."

"Sounds kind of lonely," Robyn said.

Maudlin laughed, waking the jackdaw which ruffled its feathers. "I said I must not marry. I didn't say anything about being alone."

Heat bloomed across Robyn's face.

"Retaining control means remaining strong. If you were me, would you send all the taxes to Derby and starve through the winter?"

"But they're *our* things," Robyn said.

"You are a peasant, nothing belongs to you. As the law stands, you belong to your liege lord, and that lord is me."

"The liege lord is supposed to protect us!" Robyn glared at Maudlin, who did little more than purse her lips.

"Next time you look out the window, girl, gaze upon the dozens of peasants directly under my protection. I'd be a lousy liege lord if I let them starve through the winter. I cannot protect them without extra taxes. What's left will go to Derby, as he is the Sheriff of Nottingham. He has ten times the mouths to feed as I, and he has ten times the resources."

The long soak wrinkled Robyn's fingers. "All this talk of taxes is doing my head in."

"Would you rather I use the term 'supply system'? I'm not sure why you're so against taxes. They'll benefit your father down the line."

"How's that?"

"War is expensive. The road to Jerusalem is long. The crusade may last until Christmas. Next year."

"I'm sick of war too."

"It is the way of the world," Maudlin said with a wave of her hand.

The steam rose around Robyn, softening her sore muscles, but not her sense of injustice. She felt powerless in the tub, what with being naked and slippery, she couldn't very well leap out and crack some sense into Maudlin's scone.

Maudlin said, "If you think I'm horrible, it's because I have no choice. The Earl of Derby outranks me. Prince John outranks him. The King outranks Prince John. I must answer to people who outrank me. If not, I shall be replaced with someone who will do their bidding. If you think I'm horrid, whoever takes my place will be utterly hideous, of that I'm certain."

Robyn gulped.

"Good, I'm getting through to you. I think it took longer with Marion, not that I minded."

"Stop talking about Marion!"

"And now I have your weakness. This is something you must learn, Robyn. To reveal a weakness is to reveal how your enemies can destroy you. Do you know what my weakness is?"

Robyn shrugged, barely caring any more. "You're a raving banshee?"

Laugher ricocheted around the room as Maudlin threw her head back and cackled. Rook flew off her shoulder and flapped in the air, then settled on the edge of the tub.

"You know what?" Maudlin wiped her eyes, "I am a banshee. It's one of my strengths. Own your strengths, girl. You'll need them."

By some unseen signal another maid appeared from behind a tapestry again. This one carried folded clothes.

"You will get dressed now. You have an important decision to make. Either you work for me, or you hang." Then she swept from the room in a swirl of confidence, the bird flapping to catch up and rest on her shoulder.

On shaking legs, Robyn rose from the tub and stepped into the linen sheet the maid held for her. The rough fabric dried her soaked skin. Pulling on the clothes, she felt strangely transformed. The hose was so light and soft, the long skirt heavy and draught-free, the tunic thick and warm, closing around her neck with laces to keep the heat inside and the cold out.

Which only served to confuse Robyn all the more. Being comfortable could prove addictive. Perhaps she should work for Maudlin, just for a little while? If she did, would she ever be able to break out and be herself again?

And what of Marion? Had he too been broken by an empty night on his own, then seduced with food, a hot bath and clean clothes?

Was that all it took to get a person to change sides?

Disappointment sagged her shoulders. Mentally, Robyn didn't feel broken, but she knew the cracks were there. Maudlin had merely opened them a little more. All this time she thought she'd been finding Maudlin's weakness. Instead, Robyn had revealed her own: Marion. How frustrating that Maudlin had managed to see what she could not. That she was madly in love with Marion and she hadn't even known it. Saints! She was in love with Marion.

All it had taken was to drop his name a few times and watch her squirm. Robyn had to give it to her interrogator, she was good.

"You're dressed? Good," Maudlin said as she entered the bathing room again. "It's time."

Robyn followed Maudlin to the banqueting hall. The long table was not here; nor were the high-backed chairs. Instead, someone had set a roaring fire in the hearth and placed a small table and two stools near it. An earthenware bowl filled with flatbreads took up most of the space.

"Sit," Maudlin said as she took one stool and pushed the other out with her foot. "Break bread with me and let us be friends."

Friends?

Another servant appeared. She filled two drinking tankards with water.

"Are you trying to poison me?" Robyn asked. "Not sure why you're bothering, Derby's going to hang me anyway."

"No my dear, I'm illustrating a point. What we have here is water, although not from a river." Maudlin accepted her full tankard, locked eyes with Robyn, saluted her with the mug and then drank it.

Every last drop. For acts of craziness, drinking water took things to a whole new level.

Robyn's face creased. "What's in it?"

"Nothing. That's what's so special about it." Maudlin smiled. "It's pure, clean water from a spring, not far from here. It has not touched streams or reeds. Neither fish nor frogs have spawned in it. It is pure, clean water. One can drink it straight from the ground without having to brew it as ale or cider first. Marvellous, isn't it?"

"If you say so."

"Only dirty water leads to bad humours, which in turn leads to illness and death. I plan on living for a long time yet, and this water is perfectly clean. Drink up, there's a good girl."

Eyeing the drink with suspicion, Robyn gave it a sniff. It smelled of flowers and . . . no, wait, that was her clean tunic. The water had no aroma at all, merely a faint metallic trace from the tankard.

"Taste it."

"Is this what you did to Ellen?"

Maudlin smiled and shook her head. "I did not need to. Ellen and I are linked souls. She's the daughter I never had."

"Will she inherit Sheffield when you die? Is that what you promised her?"

Maudlin opened her mouth to answer, then shut it and shook her head a little. "Drink the water."

With a "here goes nothing" attitude, she lifted the tankard to her lips and slurped some in. It tasted of . . . nothing. No remnants of anything, nothing brackish. There was something in it though, a chalkish aftertaste, but it was hard to identify because she'd never tasted anything so clean before. Liquid fresh air.

"At least I'll die happy," she said.

Maudlin took a piece of bread, tore it and offered half to Robyn. She accepted, not from being polite, but because she never turned down food.

"All water is the same," Maudlin said. "It fills bogs and streams and can turn your guts with the first sip. But place it under pressure, run it over stones, stir it up–" She raised her tankard in another salute, "–and it is made pure. The same method applies for people. They become sullied and diseased if left to stagnate. Place them under pressure, stir them up, in a manner of speaking, and they too can be made pure."

So that's what all this was about. Robyn shook her head and made a half-laugh out of a sigh. "Am I made pure now?"

"Not yet. You may have to spend a night on the stones down in the dungeon to be sure."

Robyn cast her mind to the last time been in the dungeon. It was cold, wet and hard. A night on the floor of Maudlin's timber room would be luxury in comparison.

"It's up to you," Maudlin continued. "Are you ready to work for me, with a pure heart and mind, or do you need another night to think about it?"

That's how it's done, Robyn thought, surprised at how easily she'd capitulated. Surprised at how much she wanted to work for Maudlin. If only to avoid those dungeons and keep eating good food, wearing good clothes and drinking pure water. Although . . . did Georgia or Marion have the key? Would the rest of the gang even know she was in there? If she called out through the bars they'd come and get her. Wouldn't they?

"You're thinking about your friends. Your well-meaning but misguided friends. They're all working for me now, of course."

"Really?"

"Oh yes," Maudlin looked pleased with herself, "Although, to your credit, you've taken the longest to come around."

A squawk sounded from afar. The raven flew in through an open window and landed on Maudlin's outstretched arm. "Rook, my darling, how lovely to see you again. This is Robbie, she's on our side now."

Like a talisman of evil, seeing the raven's shining eyes and sharp beak reminded Robyn of all the reasons why working for Maudlin would be so very wrong. "May I ask, Lady Maudlin, how are you to save me from the Earl of Derby?"

Maudlin's cackling laugh frightened the bird. When she composed herself, she looked Robyn directly in the eye and said, "I'm not going to tell you everything. I'm not that crazy."

CHAPTER 15

Five days later, Robyn still hadn't seen any of her friends. In a huge castle like Sheffield's, it was entirely possible they really were working for Maudlin, yet their paths had not crossed. Or they'd been put in the dungeons?

If only she and Marion had planned for this eventuality, of not seeing each other for days on end. Perhaps they already had the cow and were hiding out in the Shire Wood? That could work. Then all she had to do was escape and join them.

Adding to Robyn's woes, Ellen was here with her now, guarding her night and day. Not even the privies offered privacy, Ellen followed her in there too.

"It's all right Ellen, I can relieve myself," she said one afternoon while heading to the outhouses.

"I'd be failing in my duty if I turned my back on you. And I need to go myself, to be honest." One step behind as they walked in.

Noxious places, latrines. Most people were in and out as fast as was practical, but Ellen treated this like any other excursion. On she yapped the entire time. "It's best to keep talking when you're in here," she said to Robyn, "means you keep breathing though your mouth instead of your nose. Have you noticed how much it stinks in here?"

Robyn pulled her tunic up over her nose. The floral remnants in the fabric only made the place smell like someone had taken a dump in a rose bush.

The cold wind swirled around her naked skin as she tried to be done with her call of nature and leave.

"You think it stinks now, in summer it's even worse!" Ellen said.

Did that mean Robyn would still be here in two seasons? Not if she could help it. They would survive winter in the Shire Wood, with the cow and the carriage and they'd make it. Somehow. Although they'd need to make a new base camp because everyone knew where their hideout was by this point. Maybe back in the tower at Littleton? The walls were solid, even if the insides were a little crispy.

Finished with the privy, Robyn sorted herself and walked out. Ellen kept talking the whole time. Probably Maudlin's way of torturing her even more. As they climbed the stairs to go back inside the castle, Robyn looked out across the bailey. No sign of new arrivals.

"You're looking out for the Earl of Derby, aren't you?" Ellen asked.

How could she not? He was the one who wanted to hang her in the morning. But Maudlin had never said which morning. She'd only threatened her with imminent death and had left it at that.

"He's not here yet," Ellen said. "I won't lie to you, that's got to be a good thing. Maybe Maudlin's sent a message to him to stay home?" Ellen linked her arm through Robyn's. "I'm glad of that. I will miss you so much when you're dead."

"Thanks."

"Come on, Maudlin's waiting".

Dread weighed her down. She cast a quick look behind, to see if any of Maudlin's staff were building anything noose-friendly.

At first she saw nothing, which made her light in the head with relief. Then her stomach dipped. Roger and his men were hammering pieces of wood together. Saints! Roger probably couldn't wait to see her hang for all the trouble she'd put him through.

Ellen placed a firm hand in the middle of Robyn's back and said, "Let's not dilly dally."

Must be on my best behaviour before she wrings my neck.

"Sit down my dear," Maudlin said as they walked in to her private chambers. It was warm and inviting in here, in exactly the way a gallows wasn't. A fire in the hearth crackled away, sending out warmth and the wonderful smells of roasting pine cones.

Robyn did as she was told and sat, although Maudlin remained on her side of the room. That blasted jackdaw sat on her shoulder again. Like a second head, it was.

Another tray of fresh bread and warm cider came in, via a non-speaking peasant. At least there was an upside to this; plenty of food and drink. The bird flew towards her with a scroll in its claws. The paper dropped onto the table and threatened to roll off. Robyn caught it with one hand. The other held a chunk of bread and she wasn't letting go of that.

"What's this?"

"Our contract," Maudlin said.

Ellen interrupted, "Open it, have a look."

"That's enough, Ellen dear. Roger needs you in the bailey . . . for a construction project."

Ellen threw herself on Robyn and hugged the breath from her. "I'll miss you so much." Then she fled.

A heavy wax seal prevented the parchment from opening easily. Probably for the best if she were entrusting it to the talons of a little crow. Such a pretty seal too, in deep burgundy wax.

"Is this your coat of arms, wheat growing on a mountain?"

Maudlin made a soft chuckle. "Yes, but it's not a mountain, it's a chevron. It represents a woman at the head of the family."

Robyn wedged her thumb under the wax.

"As you know, Marion and I have been having some interesting conversations," Maudlin said.

The sound of his name seeped cold fear through Robyn's bones. "What has he told you?"

"Everything," Maudlin said with a shrug. The jackdaw, flew back to her master and rested on her shoulder. She fed it lumps of . . . something that moved a little. "I know why you resorted to becoming an outlaw. It wasn't the right thing to do, of course, but it was understandable. Your resilience is commendable, although you'll not survive winter with no shelter. Don't look so sad, of course we took the carriage back" Maudling coughed into her hand. "That Marion. He is resourceful, clever, strong. "He gets that from being a blacksmith no doubt. Naturally, I have use for a man with skills like that, and he . . . well, it turns out that even a peasant values his life in this world before meeting his maker in the next."

"Wh-what's he doing?" Robyn opened the scroll onto the table, positioning her tankard to hold it flat.

"He's re-building the tower keep you burned down."

"We never burned anything," Robyn shot back. "Roger set fire to the tower in Littleton, and the rest of Loxley. I have no idea who set fire to the tower here in Sheffield, but Marion and I were already on the ground when we saw smoke. It wasn't us."

Merriment grew in Maudlin's eyes. "I have far too many witnesses who say it was. And I have Marion's confession."

Red mist covered Robyn's eyes. It couldn't be true. It made no sense!

"Like I said, Marion has told me everything. He's smart and he values his neck. If you value yours, you'll sign your confession. Then you'll keep your neck attached to your shoulders until The Lord sees fit to call you."

The scroll was her confession? As Robyn untraveled it, she pretended to read. There were so many little markings all over it, in neat, narrow lines. A whole great block of writing with no empty spaces where her eyes could take a break. It went on forever as she kept unrolling it into her lap. Then she nudged her chair further back and kept on unravelling. The thing could have landed on the floor if she let it go. There were sections where Maudlin had joined two pieces of parchment together with bees' wax to add a further extension to the litany of crimes. Not that Robyn could read any of it, but if this were her confession, she'd committed enough for seven outlaws. At last she unfurled the final section, where she saw a series of lines, one of which had a different kind of writing on it. The raven landed on the table, a quill in her hand. Dare she reach for it?

Maudlin spoke. "Every misdemeanour and treasonous act is on your confession. All of which, as you can clearly see, is corroborated by Marion's signature. You add yours, then I shall add mine."

That was Marion's name there? The two M's, like the symbol she'd seen stamped on the helmet he'd made. The helmet he'd wanted to take on the Crusades.

"We have plenty of time, please read through the confession to show you understand the gravity of the offences you've committed."

"Read through it? But I–" Robyn pulled herself up in the nick of time. She couldn't possibly read the confession to know whether there was a grain of truth in it or not. If Marion had truly told Maudlin everything about her, then Maudlin would know by now that she couldn't read. A ray of hope shone through, like the first sunshine after the darkest winter. Maudlin didn't know Robyn couldn't read. Which meant Marion couldn't have told her everything. Had Marion told her *anything* at all? Had she been bluffing the whole time? Emboldened, Robyn pressed her point. She rolled the parchment back into a scroll and stood up.

Maudlin tilted her head. "You have not signed it."

Robyn couldn't read writing, but she was pretty good with faces. There was a tightness in Maudlin's expression that hadn't been there a moment ago. A tiny shift in power to Robyn's favour. Pushing home her advantage, she said, "You say Marion has told you everything about me?"

Maudlin's face squeezed tighter, as if she were holding things in. "Of course."

"*Absolutely* everything?"

"Everything! I'm warning you, if you don't sign that before the Earl of Derby gets here, you'll hang."

"The Earl of Derby isn't here." Robyn's heart pounded. "I don't think he's coming at all. I think you've been lying to me, not just today, but the whole time."

As if carved from stone, Maudlin's face gave nothing away.

"If Marion truly told you *everything* . . ." Robyn found herself enjoying this as she stepped closer to the fire burning warmly in the hearth. "He would have told you that I can't read."

That marble face of Maudlin's cracked. Not much, but enough to give the game away.

Warming to the topic, Robyn made her true confession. "I always wanted to read. I thought it would be a good thing to know. I used to pretend I could. But the problem with pretending is that I became so good at it, people thought I *could* read, so the few men and women in the village who could also read, never bothered to teach me because they thought I was there already. If I'd been honest from the start," her shoulders slumped at the memory, "They would have taught me. Properly."

"Or they were pretending as well," Maudlin said.

"Hadn't thought of that! Either way, Marion can read, and I can't. And if you'd been telling the truth, you would have known that. You might have found a way to get me to work for you. Or to sign to whatever's in this." Then she tossed the scroll into the fire.

Maudlin cursed. It was a word Robyn hadn't heard before, but it sounded filthy. The woman grabbed for the scroll but the bees' wax fuelled the burn.

Teasing the woman, Robyn said, "Marion is a wonderful person. If you'd listened to him, you know he's fond of making plans and thinking things through. You should have had a proper plan yourself, then this wouldn't have happened."

Maudlin tilted her head. The bird did the same. "Then you are no further use to me." She straightened her head, as did the bird. "Guards!"

From behind a tapestry—honestly, Robyn should check them out more, they made amazing hiding places—two guards appeared, each grabbing one of Robyn's arms and holding her captive.

Maudlin's eyes glistened with hatred. "Prepare the gallows!"

Icy horror zipped through Robyn. She hadn't planned for this.

"Your beloved Marion is right. Always have a backup plan," Maudlin said with a steely glare.

HANDS BOUND BEHIND HER BACK, Robyn stumbled as the

hangman lead her up the steps to the gallows. Nerves–and her hands not being where they should be–tipped her off balance.

Judging by the curves under the thick tunic, the hangman was probably a woman. Thanks to the Crusades, so many women were doing the jobs men used to do. The woman wore a hood over her face with a slit in the fabric to see through, to keep her identity secret. She was so tall too, almost as tall as–wait a minute!

Before Robyn could get another look at the woman's eyes, the hangwoman nudged her in the back. Robyn staggered forward until she stood underneath that noose. Roger must have known she'd be the one swinging, because he and whoever else was helping him had built the gallows superfast. And he was standing nearby with his group of henchmen and women, watching on with a smile on his face. At least they'd given them all a solid thumping in their last encounter. That made Robyn feel marginally better.

Another masked helper brought out a three-legged stool for Robyn to stand on. Nice touch. It looked like a milking stool, the kind Mother Eleanor used when she milked Bella. Fear churned her stomach. This was far too real now. She hoped and prayed to past and future saints that her mother was somewhere away from a window, somewhere where she wouldn't see any of this.

Robyn gulped, trying to think her way clear. Any plan at all now would be welcome, but her mind remained desperately blank. She wasn't going to die, she didn't want to. She couldn't!

"Any last words?" Maudlin said as she stroked Rook, resting on her forearm. The little crow's eyes were shiny black beads amongst the glossy feathers.

Nothing came to mind. Hardly surprising given how fast her heart whacked against her ribs, her palms perspired and her brain virtually spun inside her head. "Wait," she suddenly thought of something. "The Earl of Derby has to be here."

"Did I not tell you?" Maudlin said with a calculated smile. "He sent his apologies. Terribly busy hanging more traitors in Nottingham."

Guilt and fear twisted her gut. "Like who?"

"Nobody you need concern yourself with," Maudlin said as she turned to address the crowd milling about them. "We have before us a traitor to the King! She will be hanged, not merely for her terrible deeds, but to serve as a warming to all that treason and theft of property will never be tolerated."

"You can steal from us but we can't take it back, we have to come here and beg for scraps from the table!"

The crowd murmured.

Maudlin yelled, "Quiet!"

The crowd shut up.

Robyn didn't care. "At least I got a hot bath out of it!"

The crowd laughed.

Emboldened by their response, Robyn said, "What's more, I think your hangman could use one, he stinks!"

The crowd roared with laughter. The hangwoman–Robyn was sure it was a woman–sniffed the armpits of her tunic. The crowd laughed even more.

"Shut up, the lot of you!" Maudlin cried out. The jackdaw flapped to keep her balance. "One more peep and I'll hang the lot of you!"

"Then who'll do all your work?" Robyn grew reckless. It had to be the insane fear of imminent death making her behave like this. "You hardly do any work at all! All you do is eat all the food and take hot baths!" Not exactly true, but at this stage of the game it didn't matter.

Sure enough, the crowd laughed again. People began throwing rotten turnips and mouldy bread, not at Robyn but Maudlin. Rook took wing and flew to a rooftop.

Something burned with clarity in Robyn's mind. "You need us. That's your weakness!" She cried out. "You treat people like dirt. Less than dirt. But your true weakness is that you need people. You can't threaten us or make us do anything anymore bec–"

A noose slipped around her neck. The hangwoman pulled it tight.

Maudlin turned on Robyn, but she kept her voice loud enough for the crowd to hear. "You're right, of course. I cannot hang *everyone*. But I can hang you!"

The hangwoman–strong woman that she was–lifted Robyn bodily onto the stool. The crowd fell to silence. Heart rattling against her ribs, Robyn's breath came in short bursts. The hang-woman tightened the rope above her, making Robyn stand on tip-toes to ease the pressure. How much would this hurt when they kicked the stool out from underneath? Please let this be swift. Tears spritzed from her eyes as she searched the crowd for Marion. What a fool she'd been to never tell him she loved him. Now it was too late.

"I have something important to say!" She wheezed out. That rope sure was tight. "I go now to meet the almighty with a pure heart and a clear conscience, which is more than I can say for Maudlin, who is responsible for your suffering!"

Arrows rained through the air. Something tugged behind Robyn and her hands sprang free from their binding. The noose, however, remained firmly around her neck. She reached up to loosen it just as everything went mad. Someone kicked the stool away. Robyn braced herself for the pain in her neck, only to find her body falling hard on the gallows platform, landing nose-first. Her hands grabbed at the rope, loosening it enough to rip it over her head. She was free. Sticky warmth spread over her face. She touched her aching nose to find it covered in blood. The sharp pain made her eyes water and her ears ring. But she was alive!

Mayhem filled the world as people shouted and ran in all direc-tions. Suddenly, Marion was there in front of her, lifting her back to her feet.

"You took your time," she said through the pain.

"No points for improvising?" He grinned and made her heart flip.

Relief, and the sheer joy of being alive crashed over Robyn. "I love you, you know."

Marion winked at her and threw the noose away so it couldn't be re-used. "Feeling's mutual. But if you don't mind, can we save the kissing for later? What with all this—" He made a circling motion with his hand around her nose.

"Yeah." Urgh, her face must be mashed with blood. "I totally planned this: this is exactly what was supposed to happen."

"And an excellent plan it was too," Marion said. "Now, at the risk of getting my head bitten off, what's next?"

"Easy," Robyn grinned as if the battle were already won. "We high tail it back to the Shire Wood and live in peace with nature."

"I like it." Marion stepped away suddenly, pulled an arrow from his quiver and fired it into the air–the arrow flew straight into the wing of Rook the jackdaw, bringing her down. The bird would be maimed and possibly never fly again. "I totally meant to do that."

Maudlin screamed and ran for Rook. Squawks and screams filled the air.

"Or," Marion said, aiming an arrow at Maudlin, but not setting it loose, "We could defeat Maudlin, shove her in the dungeons and stay in Sheffield until winter is over."

Defenceless, Maudlin cradled the injured Rook in one arm and raised the other, palm outward in defeat. Things became very still and quiet as people realised what was going on. Maudlin, their liege lord, was . . . *capitulating*?

Robyn wiped the blood from her face. It hurt just to touch her nose.

"Surrender!" Marion said.

Maudlin said nothing.

A battle cry sounded from across the bailey. It was Ellen leading Roger and his rag-tag men into the arena.

With fresh weapons.

"Don't take your eyes off Maudlin," Robyn warned Marion as she leapt into the fray. Beside her was Joan and Georgia, they had a spare longstaff so she could join in.

"You make a terrible hangman," Robyn said as she stood beside Georgia.

Twack, biff, thump, dodge, parry, thrust.

"How did you know it was me?"

Bash, bang, oof!

"If it wasn't you, I'd be dead."

"Fair point."

Whack, whump.

"You two, pay attention, we have a fight on our hands." Joan said.

Thump, thwack, biff, grunt!

It felt good to get all the aggro out, especially taking on Roger who had caused them so much trouble right from the start. Perhaps her father was doing something similar, battling in the Crusades right now. With a few more biffs and bashes, Joan, Georgia and Robyn had Roger and his gang moaning on the ground, begging for mercy.

"This is all your fault, Doncaster," Robyn said. "If you hadn't been so brutal in the first place, we would have paid up and stayed where we were in Loxley. But you had to get greedy."

"I have a family too," he said, holding his forearm over his face to deflect any more blows.

"You're lucky I don't like hitting someone when they're already down," Robyn said. "Justify it all you want, but this," she waved her arm at the chaos around them, "is on your head."

Some of Roger's henchfolk got to their feet and dropped whatever they were using for weapons.

"We surrender. Can we join you now?" One of them said.

Another pleaded. "You said we could, back in the Shire Wood."

That she had. "OK then. Take Roger and whoever is still loyal to him to the dungeons." Robyn looked about to see who exactly would remain loyal to a tax collector. Nobody, it seemed. "Good. I'm going after Ellen."

Ellen was scarpering towards the burnt-out tower. Robyn gave pursuit. Maudlin was barrelling for them both and Marion was right behind with his arrow ready.

"Out of my way!" Maudlin charged past, pushing Robyn into a puddle.

Marion too ran past. Robyn jumped back to her feet, ran to a barrel of water and washed the blood from her face, then she took off after Marion, Maudlin and Ellen. Every muscle burned as she took to the steps two at a time up the tower.

Gasping for breath, lungs tight with pain, she reached the top floor. Ellen stood in some kind of basket, attached to a pulley system and plenty of ropes. Ropes that went . . . where exactly?

"Always have a back-up plan," Maudlin said, stepping in to the basket with Ellen and setting them free.

Zip! The basket slid downwards with Ellen and Maudlin in it, over the moat and into the woods beyond.

Robyn grabbed Marion's bow out of his hand and ripped an arrow from his quiver. She fired. The arrow sailed through the air and pierced Maudlin's arm.

The woman screamed in pain. Not a kill shot, merely a match for the raven. Robyn loosed another arrow, but it flew over their heads as they dropped out of sight.

Furious, Robyn grabbed for Marion's knife and sawed at the rope.

"No! Stop!" Marion grabbed her hand away.

"But they're getting away!" Robyn cried.

"Cut the drawstring on the bow instead."

Confusion slowed her for a second. Marion grabbed her knife and cut the string with a sharp "twang". Then he slotted the bow over the rope and held on to the sides.

"Hold on to me!" He shouted.

Robyn locked her arms around Marion's shoulders and hung on.

Shhhhhrrrrrrrr! They swished down the length of the rope, the icy north wind freezing their necks and ripping their howls of terror away.

On the opposite side, Ellen hacked at the end of the rope, attached to a tree.

They weren't going to make it.

The river below promised an icy fall.

Ellen kept hacking. Maudlin hobbled away to the north with her raven.

Nearly over the river. Nearly . . . nearly. *Riiiip!* The last fibres of rope tore apart. Robyn and Marion dropped away, landing heavily on the river bank. Half in, half out of the water, completely covered in pain. Winded from the fall, Robyn took a second to drag air into her lungs. Then she pulled her legs out of the water and crawled onto the grassy bank, helping Marion out at the same time.

He curled his legs up under him and looked like a freshly-landed fish, his mouth opening and closing so much. Robyn dragged a breath over the pain and got her body working again. "Breathe, Marion, Saints alive, breathe."

He uncurled his legs and pulled a breath in. Then another. His wincing expression eventually softened. "What happened?"

Failure swamped Robyn. "They got away." She looked towards the trees. "That way."

"No, I mean, with the rope. Did it break?"

Huh? "Ellen cut it."

"Oh, so our end held up?" He sat up and edged closer to her, checking her face and body for breaks.

"I'm fine, just sore. Didn't you see Ellen cutting the rope?"

With a shake of his head he said, "Had my eyes closed the whole time."

Robyn threw her arms around him and cried. "They got away."

"We'll get them next time, don't worry." Marion returned the hug.

They hugged for a while, then the hug turned into rubbing their backs and arms to keep warm. A howl of frustration broke free. If they hadn't cut the string on the bow she could have fired on Ellen, if not both of them.

But then she remembered something amazing. "You hate heights."

"Yep."

"You hate heights but you got us both down here from all the way up there!"

A grin formed. "I guess I did."

"Have I mentioned lately how much I love you?" Robyn kissed him, her cold lips meeting his, both thawing mighty fast under the onslaught of emotions roaring through her. Their feet may be freezing, their pants wet, her nose on fire from the pain, but the rest of their bodies were toasty hot.

"I didn't believe what Maudlin said about you," Robyn said.

"And never for a second did I think you said the things she said you did either." Marion replied.

"Wait, what?" Robyn recounted the sentence in her mind and lost track. "What did she tell you about me?"

"She said you'd confessed everything and that you'd hang. Or I could take your place."

Cold shivers stole into Robyn's body. "That was your signature on the confession?"

"Yeah."

"You were going to hang in my place?"

"I was hoping it wouldn't come to that. And it didn't, so, you know, it's all good."

"My darling Marion," Robyn covered him in fresh kisses. "I would never have let you do that."

"I wasn't sure what was going to happen, but then Will, Joan and Georgia broke me out and all we had to do was take up our positions near the gibbet and wait for you to be brought out."

Tears broke free. Robyn gulped in a lungful of air as she buried her head into Marion's chest, gently, because her nose still screamed in pain. "I'm going to have nightmares about this for years."

"It's all right," he stroked her hair and rubbed her back. It felt so soothing and calming, she started to breathe more normally. "It didn't come to that. You know that Joan, Georgia and Will are always going to be in your corner."

Relief, fear, gratitude; it all mixed together in an incoherent bubble of tears and laughter.

Eventually Marion got to his feet and helped Robyn to hers. "I have a plan."

"You do?"

"Yes. Let's go someplace warmer."

"I like that plan. It's a good one."

By the time they'd walked around to the Sheffield gatehouse, the rest of the battle was pretty much over. They were at the mopping up stage. The peasants of Sheffield, seeing Maudlin and Ellen gone, were only too happy to break the gallows apart to use for fire wood.

Roger was below stairs in the dungeons.

Shivering at the memory of those cold cells, Robyn felt it was an apt punishment. At least he wouldn't be homeless for winter, and unlike their cottages back home, stone dungeons didn't burn. The man was getting off lightly.

"I have a plan too," Robyn said. "Let's get the fires going in the kitchens and cook up a feast for everyone."

"I like that plan," Marion said as they surveyed the remains of the melee around them. "But I didn't know you could cook."

"I can't," Robyn confessed, "But I'm sure someone here can."

"Here's the treasury," Wilfred said as he and Madge came forth, their aprons filled with trinkets, coins, goblets and all sorts of goodies.

The crowd went crazy and cheered, then they mobbed Wilfred and Madge. At first Robyn thought they'd be trampled in the stampede, but the crowd wasn't interested in the loot, they wanted to thank them for getting it all back. In the crush, Wilfred and Madge's treasures fell all over the ground.

"That could buy a lot of pies," Robyn said.

"We'll need it," Marion said. "Thanks to Roger's mess, every villager for miles around will descend on Sheffield, wanting shelter for the winter."

"We should make Roger look after them, he's the one who burned down their houses."

Marion smiled as he shared the conspiracy with her. "I like the way you think."

EPILOGUE

"I'm still cross Maudlin got away," Robyn kicked the ground as she walked beside Shadow and Plus One into the Shire Wood. Snow fell in soft drifts around them, the icy wind bit the tips of her fingers off.

"She'll be in all kinds of misery, don't you worry," Marion said, reaching for her hand to give it a comforting squeeze. "You're frozen, why didn't you say something?"

"Too busy being cross," Robyn said with a shrug.

"Come here." Marion wrapped both her hands in his, then breathed on them. Thick steam rose from his lips.

"Do you think they've gone to our old camp?" She asked.

"Anything's possible, but they'd probably want to get as far from Sheffield as they can." He said. "Maybe they've gone to Nottingham and thrown themselves at Derby's mercy?"

"Do you think we'll ever see her again?"

"Sure we will. Maudlin's the kind of woman who bears a grudge."

Shadow and Plus One stopped to sniff at a green pine seedling poking through the snow. In a few weeks, the snow would be so deep there would be no green at all.

"Right. So, what's our plan?"

Marion grinned. "Do I really sound like that?"

"Pretty much."

"I'm insufferable." He flashed her a grin and followed it with a wink.

"We-e-e-ll, you're not exactly insufferable. Not all the time at any rate."

"Thank goodness for that. Now, where's the axe?"

"On the back of Plus One."

"That's her name all the time now?" Marion asked.

"It kind of suits her."

"Poor horse." Marion took the axe and checked the blade, making sure it was clean and sharp. In the Shire Wood, the big trees would take an effort to cut down, but they would burn for longer than the thinner branches.

"That one's pretty good," Robyn pointed to a mid-sized tree. "At the risk of sounding insufferable, may I suggest a plan?"

"You're going to keep rubbing that in, aren't you?"

"At every opportunity," this time Robyn gave Marion a wink and a grin. "Why don't we take turns in whacking the tree, then we'll get it down in half the time."

"Or, at the risk of sounding even more insufferable," Marion looked like he was really enjoying himself. "We take a tree each and fell two in the same time. Unless you're not strong enough to bring down a whole tree by yourself."

Robyn took the bait. "I'll take this tree, you find your own."

"This is my tree, I'm closest to it." Marion made ready to swing.

"Or," Robyn interrupted and Marion missed his mark, the axe striking at a bad angle and barely making a dent. "You chop the trees, then I chop the branches off when we fell it."

"A dizzying array of options," Marion swung truly and made a hefty slice into the trunk. Another whack sent a wedge of wood flying out.

"Honestly, I could stand here and plan all day," Robyn said.

"Fine by me," Marion swung the axe, creating a sizeable wedge in the tree. "But then again–" *thwack* "–You'll freeze if you don't–" *hack* "swing into action soon. You know the old saying, 'Cut your own firewood and it warms you twice'."

Watching him swing that axe warmed Robin all the way

through anyway. She picked a mid-sized tree a few paces away and smudged the bark with mud to give her something to aim at. *Thwack! Grunt. Swing, thunk!* Four swings in, her muscles burned with pain. Her shoulders felt ready to fall off. She'd barely made a dent in the tree. Marion had already carved a pie-sliced wedge right through to the middle of his tree. Now he turned the axe around and swung with the blunt side of it into the wood, just above the cut. The tree wobbled as it creaked and groaned. He whacked it again; the trunk split to the side and crashed down.

"You are so amazing right now," Robyn said.

They both grinned as the snow fell in thick blobs. Marion walked over to Robyn's tree, a tree that didn't look in danger of falling any time soon.

"Let's take it in turns then," he said as he hefted his axe.

In companionable silence, they hacked and cut their way through this one. Despite both of them working together, this one took longer than the first to bring down.

"I think I picked the wrong kind of tree." Robyn said.

"It's an oak," Marion said after taking his swing. "We'll not be through this before Christmas."

"What sort did you cut down?"

"Think it was a birch. Bit easier on the arms than this."

"I have an idea." Leaping into action, Robyn climbed up the tree, scaling the branches like a ladder. "Throw me the rope."

"OK, whatever the lady wants." Marion threw the coil of rope towards her. "You know if you'd planned this, you could have tied the rope to you in the first place before you climbed up there."

"Shut it. I'm getting the job done." Her fingers fumbled as she tied the end of the rope high up around the top branches and trunk. "Right, take the end of it. Tie it to the horses, get them to pull the tree over."

The horses stood well out of the way, under the boughs of a fur tree, which kept its needles even in the depths of winter. Robyn scrambled down the tree, her fingers burning from the cold. How beautiful would an open fire be right about now?

"I get it," Marion tied the rope to the back of Shadow's harness, then rubbed the horse's neck to calm and soothe her.

Shadow was having none of it and whinnied her displeasure. Even though the horses had thick hairy coats, they must be freezing too.

"Marion, you whack through the other side of the tree, I'll hold Shadow steady so we can pull it over and get it down sooner."

Creak, thwack!

Groan, riiiiiiip crash!

"We did it!" Overjoyed with success, Robyn grabbed Marion in a fierce hug which ended with them giggling and kissing in the snow.

"We got a whole two trees down."

"Yeah." Robyn was exhausted already.

"There's not much daylight left, we'd better get them back."

For all their effort, it looked pretty measly. They'd have to come back early tomorrow, and the next day, and the next to have a hope of keeping the people of Sheffield warm through the rest of winter.

Noises and singing came from between the trees. Turning, they saw Joan, Georgia, Wilfred and Madge approaching. They had axes and ropes in their hands and smiles on their faces.

"What are you doing here?" Robyn asked.

"We couldn't let you do this on your own," Joan said, "We're a team!"

The sight of her team filled Robyn with sunshine. Soon the forest rang with sounds of thwacking axes and falling trees. In no time, the others strapped the trunks together and urged the horses to drag them towards the castle.

"Race you back," Robyn said, tearing off from Marion.

"Hey wait!" he shouted.

Their breaths came out in thick misty puffs, their faces pink and flushed from exertion. On they ran, for the sheer joy of being alive and being happy. Robyn was in the lead, holding the front of her frock off the ground to stop her from tripping. Marion closed the gap, laughing as he tried to catch her.

She was laughing so hard she couldn't keep running, the hem of her skirt soaked with melted snow.

They both looked wild and a little bit crazy. Near the gates, they snuggled for warmth, waiting for the others to arrive back with the horses and the larger trees for burning.

"What's that?" Robyn pointed to a small fir tree Joan carried with her.

"I thought it would be nice to have something green to decorate the bailey."

Once through the castle gates, Robyn and Marion took in the bustling scene. By the kitchens near *The Unicorn*, Mother Eleanor milked a cow they didn't recognise. Somebody else close by milked Bella, listening to Eleanor's helpful instructions. Everything looked busy and settled, everyone had something to do to help get them through the cold months ahead.

As Marion had predicted, in the past few weeks people from outlying villages had come to Sheffield for shelter and protection. The castle was packed. As each new group came, they brought with them small supplies of food, blankets, animal skins and live animals as well. Eleanor was in her element teaching young boys and girls how to milk the cows, while Joan's elderly parents showed folks how to make warm nesting boxes for the chickens so they'd have a steady supply of eggs.

Snow continued to fall, coating the bailey in a blanket of magic. Here and there small fires burned in braziers. People huddled around them, keeping warm. Robin noticed their furtive glances, because they wanted to know what they should do next. What did they do next? She'd think of something soon. With Marion's help. And Will's and Madge's and Joan's and Georgia's. And even her mother's help, if she could get her away from the cows for any length of time.

Marion put his arm around Robyn's shoulders and guided her to the stairs of the old tower. Burnt patches were still visible on the walls, but the smoky smell was mostly gone now.

"I have a surprise for you," he whispered.

They climbed the stairs to the landing and Marion reached behind a tapestry. Those tapestries were marvellous for hiding things! He held out the re-strung bow and gave it to her.

"You fixed it!" Admiring the craftwork, she held the bow and pulled the string back, loving the tension and the strength of it. "Thank you so much!"

"I'm not sure how much use we'll get out of it, but I wanted to fix it for you," Marion said.

A grin formed. "You sneaky thing. I had no idea you'd done this. Thank you so much." She kissed and hugged him tightly.

"I'll fix more things if this is how you thank me."

She gave him another kiss for good measure. It warmed her all the way to her boots. "Interesting." Robyn said, full of curiosity. "When I kiss you, I warm up. Have you ever noticed that happening to you?"

"I was just thinking that myself. Might need to try it again and test it though." Marion's kiss made her heart beat way too fast from the sheer joy of it.

Eventually they broke away. Through a grin, Robyn said, "Kissing is a very good way to stay warm in winter."

Marion snuck in one more kiss. "That is a brilliant plan."

* The End *

AUTHOR'S NOTE

I have been a fan of the Robin Hood legend for as long as I can remember. I've loved the various movies and TV series, especially the 1980s British version starring Michael Praed. (Showing my age here.) I also loved the reboot with Jonas Armstrong, Lucy Griffiths and Richard (swoon) Armitage. All that leather! Yowzers!

But it always bothered me that there was only one girl in the story, Marian. This never sat well with me, as all my friends growing up happened to be girls. That meant we couldn't 'play' Robin Hood because we couldn't all be Marian, right?

Where was our female folk hero?

Historically, the time Robin was supposed to be 'robbing from the rich and giving to the poor' was around the 1190s. History tells us Prince John (Boo! Hiss!) was regent of England while his older brother King Richard (The Lionheart) was off fighting the first of many crusades.

King Richard wasn't on his own, he had a whole army with him. Armies made of strapping young men, with their families in tow to source food, cook meals, tend the wounded, make and repair armour and so on.

So why, every time there was an adaptation of the Robyn Hood legend, the forest of 'Sherwood' in England is full of healthy, able-bodied blokes? Those blokes should have been on the Crusades as well.

Marion used to be a common boy's name. It meant 'son of Mary' and was incredibly popular until the early 20th century. It fell out of favour around 1922, when a massively successful movie of Robin Hood, starring Douglas Fairbanks, was released. The next Robyn Hood movie in the 1930s, starring Errol Flynn and Olivia de Havilland, felt like the nail in the coffin for Marion as a boy's name.

The most famous male Marion would probably be John Wayne, who was born Marion Morrison, in 1907. His first screen credit was in 1929, as 'Duke Morrison". He became John Wayne for his 1930 role in The Big Trail.

But enough mining Wikipedia for information. I love history, and I know women played a much bigger role than we're led to believe. After all, if not for women, we wouldn't actually be here. If you think about it, at the time of Robyn's exploits, just about everyone except for royalty and the clergy were illiterate. People told news and shared stories verbally or with paintings, so it's easy to understand why a flutterby later came to be called a butterfly, and a norange was slowly turned into an orange. Pies made of umbles (offal) became 'humble pie' and earned an idiom to go with it.

If you have a listen to the names of Robyn's 'merry band' so many of the crew sound like women. Allan a'Dale is easily Ellen. George a'Green is Georgia Green, Robyn is such a girl's name and as I've already said, Marion is totally a boy. The rest of the roles all fell into place. Little John was clearly Joan, from a hamlet called Littleton. Much is Madge. (Some stories have Midge for Much, but this too could still be a woman.)

But who was Friar Tuck? It had to be Robyn's mum, the 'mother hen' of the group, advising them to keep nice and 'tie their frocks'. Will Scarlet, however, didn't undergo gender re-assignment. He also wouldn't have worn much red in real life, not in the green and brown forest where he would have stood out like a beacon. No, he's red because of his allergies (which were a totally new thing in the 1190s.)

When it did come time to write the stories of Robyn's outlaws down, to share them widely, the times had changed. Two hundred years had passed. That's plenty of time for the names and tales to get muddled up. Old stories were looked at through contemporary eyes, altered to fit the prevailing moods and tastes of the time. Who were the writers? Royalty and monks. Mostly blokes. They wrote about what they knew, and they wedged a religious sort in there (Friar Tuck) to make sure Robin's soul didn't burn in the fires of everlasting hell. Or they simply loved the idea of having a kick-arse monk, because religious clerics yearned for adventures themselves.

My deep and abiding love for history couldn't help sneaking into this book. I was shocked, shocked I tell you, to discover that nobody called the particular wooded area of England 'Sherwood Forest' until the 1800s. Earlier than that the region was referred to as the Shire Wood. I loved it, so I used it.

Although I was playing with history, I wanted the characters' daily lives to feel authentic. They couldn't jump in a car and drive to Nottingham, but digital maps showed me how far someone could reasonably walk (or ride a horse) in one day. How convenient, Sheffield is a day's walk from Loxley!

Of yet more interest was the city and castle of Sheffield itself. This was one of the first castles in England to be reinforced with stone walls. Prior to about 1150, most castles in England (and these were mott and bailey-style buildings consisting of a single tower and a big fence around a flattened bailey, or yard) were made from timber. They burned magnificently when under attack, and had to be rebuilt.

Imagine my utter delight to discover a very real Maud of Sheffield! The real Maud was born in the 1170s in Sheffield itself. She was the only surviving child of the Lord of Hallamshire and the last of the De Lovetots. I lost days to researching the people of the time, but it was so much fun. In my story, Maud remains unmarried and therefore retains control of the castle estate. In real life, she was married off and had six surviving children. Her husband joined one of the later crusades, and was never seen again. Secretly I think Maud wanted it that way.

Yes, I donate every year to the Wikipedia appeal, because Wikipedia is so very useful.

ABOUT THE AUTHOR

Ebony McKenna is the author of the ONDINE series, about a teen whose pet ferret starts talking with a Scottish accent.

The titles in reading order are:

The Summer of Shambles

The Autumn Palace

The Winter of Magic

The Spring Revolution

Other works:

1916-ish

Novellas:

Lara's Christmas Gamble (set in Ondine's world of Brugel)

Dangerous Honesty (from the anthology Dangerous Boys)

www.ebonymckenna.com

If you enjoyed this novel, please tell your friends or leave a review on your book review website of choice.

Thank you.